PENGUIN BOOKS
THE CREATION

Ernst Haas was born in Vienna in 1921. He attended medical school; but his artistic inclinations soon led him to photography, and he presented his first one-man show in 1947. In 1950 *Life* magazine devoted a history-making twenty-four pages in color to his essay on New York. This was followed by a photographic report on Paris, which included some of the first of his famous studies of motion. Since then, his pictures, taken all over the world, have appeared in magazines on both sides of the Atlantic. His work has been shown in New York at the Museum of Modern Art, the Gallery of Modern Art, Asia House, and the IBM Gallery. His book *In America* is a unique collection of photographs of this country's natural phenomena, man-made creations, and people. Mr. Haas died in 1986.

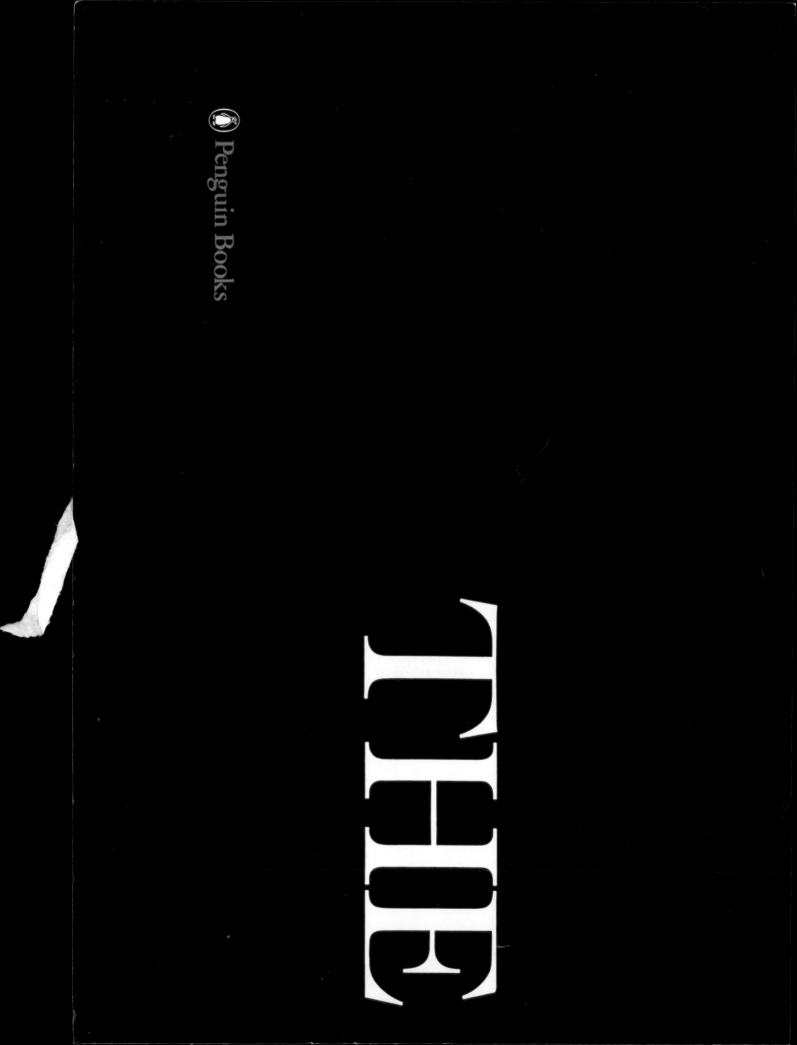

CREATION

ERNST HAAS

PENGUIN BOOKS
Published by the Penguin Group
Viking Penguin Inc., 40 West 23rd Street,
New York, New York 10010, U.S.A.
Penguin Books Ltd, 27 Wrights Lane, London W8 5TZ, England

Penguin Books Australia Ltd, Ringwood,
Victoria, Australia
Penguin Books Canada Limited, 2801 John Street,
Markham, Ontario, Canada L3R 1B4
Penguin Books (N.Z.) Ltd, 182–190 Wairau Road,
Auckland 10, New Zealand

Penguin Books Ltd, Registered Offices: Harmondsworth,
Middlesex, England

First published in the United States of America by The Viking Press 1971
First published in Great Britain by Michael Joseph, Ltd, 1971
Published in Penguin Books 1976
Reprinted 1977, 1978, 1981
Reissued 1988

LIBRARY OF CONGRESS CATALOGING IN PUBLICATION DATA
Haas, Ernst, 1921–1986
The creation.
1. Color photography. 2. Photography, Artistic. 3. Creation. I. Title.
TR510.H25   1976   779'.3   76-18761
ISBN 0 14 00.4284 9

Printed in Japan by Dai Nippon Printing Co., Ltd, Tokyo
Set in Garamond Bold #3

CONTENTS

In moments of truth we ask ourselves the eternal questions: Why are we here? Where did we come from? What is the reason for all existence?

Contemporary intelligence finds it hard to accept that man was created, suddenly, as a separate entity. A more popular belief is that organic life grew and developed by itself, and that man gradually evolved. The first approach, as presented in Genesis, is poetic, and the other, perhaps, more scientific. Yet, lacking evidence that an animal has ever shown signs of human consciousness, we stand somewhere between the two philosophies: original creation and evolution. If we believe that the whole of creation was an accident; if it was meant, then we are part of that meaning.

However much we try to rebel against nature, we cannot escape being a part of it. The elements that surround us also flow through us; and the cycle of human life bears a close relationship to the span of the four seasons. The one faculty that distinguishes us from other creatures is a brain that offers us the opportunity of free choice.

In this present age of science, at once so powerfully constructive and destructive, we seek instinc-

tively to defend ourselves by searching for the elemental, the natural, the absolute, the universal. But in our desire to discover, to know, and to label all the columns that support the roof of our existence we realize that one link must always remain an enigma. The idea of the beginning, of something originating out of nothing, of existence born out of nonexistence, remains beyond human comprehension. Science, while enlarging our view of the solar system, has never solved the mystery of the universe itself. This quest, a spiritual one, has always been within the realm of religion and of the highest forms of art and literature.

In his endeavor to remake himself and to remake his world, man is confronted with the cruel truth that his intelligence frequently works against instinct and that out of greed he mistreats what was given to him in trust.

Never has youth been obliged to take greater interest in what science on the one hand and the wisdom of the ages on the other have to offer for the future welfare of mankind. And the cause of responsive members of the new generation has become to effect a better balance between materialism and the affairs of the spirit. In their own idealistic and energetic way, they are struggling to establish a simpler concept and conduct of life, nearer to nature, since nature remains the source of all new beginnings.

If truth is what we believe to be true, then every period, every culture, has created its own truth, which has always been deeply rooted in man's concept of the reason for existence. But in extreme situations, such as pain, love, or joy, man reaches from the narrower fact of truth into the broader dimensions of poetry to express better all that he feels, sees, and believes.

In the first chapter of Genesis we find a related situation, where the unknown is given credence through poetic vision. Today the abstract idea of the beginning of the world still lives in all of us, filling us with a longing to understand how it came about.

In Genesis the implications are so deep and far-reaching that it seems miraculous that so much can be said in so few words, and in such simple ones. To read the moving passages in the first page of the Old Testament is to expose one's mind to a constant flow of images: light, darkness, movement, color, space, power; the conflict and union of opposing elements; the birth of the earth and the coming of the seasons; the emergence of vegetation, fish, fowl, animals; and eventually

the crowning of the evolutionary pyramid, the birth of man.

Myths, the religious answers to questions about the beginning, are to be found in many cultures. The Bible story of the Creation is most familiar to readers in the West, but the theme recurs in most scriptures, notably the Egyptian and Babylonian and the Rig Veda of the Hindus. In addition there are the creeds of cultures without scriptures—the American Indian, for example. This is based firmly on nature, the elements and the seasons, incorporating rituals that draw freely, simply, and beautifully on the whole concept of creation and re-creation.

"In the beginning God created the heaven and the earth." The opening statement of Genesis induces in one an immediate sense of awe, and of humility. It was in such a mood that this book was begun, and in which the finished work is presented here. No claim should be made for it other than that it represents a sort of "spiritual ecology" in praise of the earth which man inherited and should seek ardently to protect.

William Blake saw "the world in a grain of sand." It can be seen in many such things, for in the smallest cells are reflections of the largest. And in photography, through an interplay of scales, a whole universe within a universe can be revealed. This has been attempted both in the selection of the pictures on the following pages and in the particular way that they have been arranged.

A recurring phrase in "The Creation" is: "And God saw that it was good." It is hoped that this book may prove that it is still "good," and suggest that it can remain good if only man will appreciate what he has far too long taken for granted.

In the beginning God created the heaven and the earth.

And the earth was without form, and void; and darkness was upon the face of the deep. And the Spirit of God moved upon the face of the waters.

And God said, Let there be light: and there was light.

And God saw the light, that it was good: and God divided the light from the darkness.

And God called the light Day, and the darkness he called Night. And the evening and the morning were the first day.

And God said, Let there be a firmament in the midst of the waters, and let it divide the waters from the waters.

And God made the firmament, and divided the waters which were under the firmament from the waters which were above the firmament: and it was so.

And God called the firmament Heaven. And the evening and the morning were the second day.

And God said, Let the waters under the heaven be gathered together unto one place, and let the dry land appear: and it was so.

And God called the dry land Earth; and the gathering together of the waters called he Seas: and God saw that it was good.

And God said, Let the earth bring forth

grass, the herb yielding seed, and the fruit tree yielding fruit after his kind, whose seed is in itself, upon the earth: and it was so.

And the earth brought forth grass, and herb yielding seed after his kind, and the tree yielding fruit, whose seed was in itself, after his kind: and God saw that it was good.

And the evening and the morning were the third day.

And God said, Let there be lights in the

firmament of the heaven to divide the day
from the night; and let them be for signs, and
for seasons, and for days, and years:

And let them be for lights in the firmament
of the heaven to give light upon the earth: and
it was so.

And God made two great lights; the
greater light to rule the day, and the lesser
light to rule the night: he made the stars also.

And God set them in the firmament of the

heaven to give light upon the earth,

And to rule over the day and over the night,
and to divide the light from the darkness: and
God saw that it was good.

And the evening and the morning were
the fourth day.

And God said, Let the waters bring forth
abundantly the moving creature that hath
life, and fowl that may fly above the earth in
the open firmament of heaven.

And God created great whales, and every living creature that moveth, which the waters brought forth abundantly, after their kind, and every winged fowl after his kind: and God saw that it was good.

And God blessed them, saying, Be fruitful, and multiply, and fill the waters in the seas, and let fowl multiply in the earth.

And the evening and the morning were the fifth day.

And God said, Let the earth bring forth the living creature after his kind, cattle, and creeping thing, and beast of the earth after his kind: and it was so.

And God made the beast of the earth after his kind, and cattle after their kind, and every thing that creepeth upon the earth after his kind: and God saw that it was good.

And God said, Let us make man in our image, after our likeness: and let them have dominion over the fish of the sea, and over the fowl of the air; and over the cattle, and over all the earth, and over every creeping thing that creepeth upon the earth.

So God created man in his own image, in the image of God created he him; male and female created he them.

And God blessed them, and God said unto them, Be fruitful, and multiply, and replenish the earth, and subdue it: and have dominion over the fish of the sea, and over the fowl of the air, and over every living thing that moveth upon the earth.

And God said, Behold, I have given you every herb bearing seed, which is upon the face of all the earth, and every tree, in the which is the fruit of a tree yielding seed; to you it shall be for meat.

And to every beast of the earth, and to every fowl of the air, and to every thing that

creepeth upon the earth, wherein there is life,
I have given every green herb for meat: and
it was so.

And God saw every thing that he had
made, and, behold, it was very good. And the
evening and the morning were the sixth day.

Thus the heavens and the earth were
finished, and all the host of them.

And on the seventh day God ended his
work which he had made; and he rested on

the seventh day from all his work which he had made.

And God blessed the seventh day, and sanctified it: because that in it he had rested from all his work which God created and made.

These are the generations of the heavens and of the earth when they were created, in the day that the Lord God made the earth and the heavens.

And every plant of the field before it was in the earth, and every herb of the field before it grew: for the Lord God had not caused it to rain upon the earth, and there was not a man to till the ground.

But there went up a mist from the earth, and watered the whole face of the ground. And the Lord God formed man of the dust of the ground, and breathed into his nostrils the breath of life and man became a living soul..

The Elements

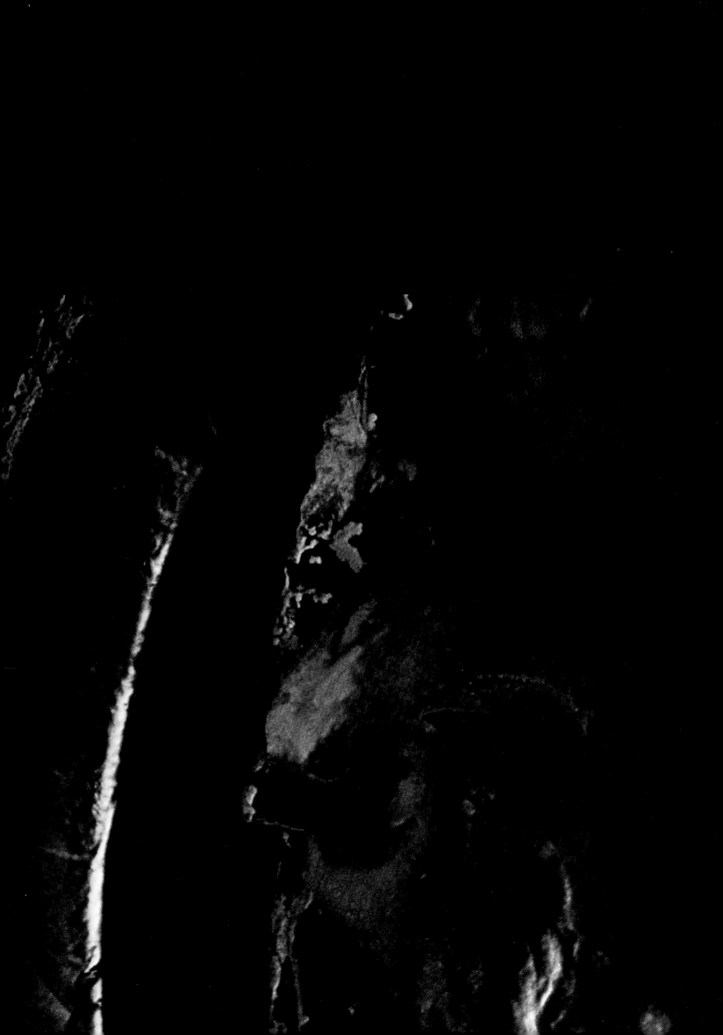

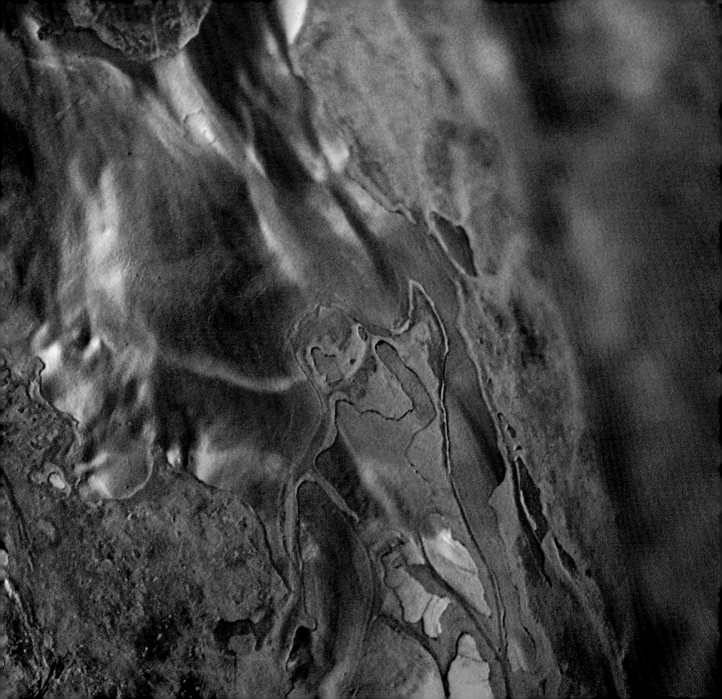

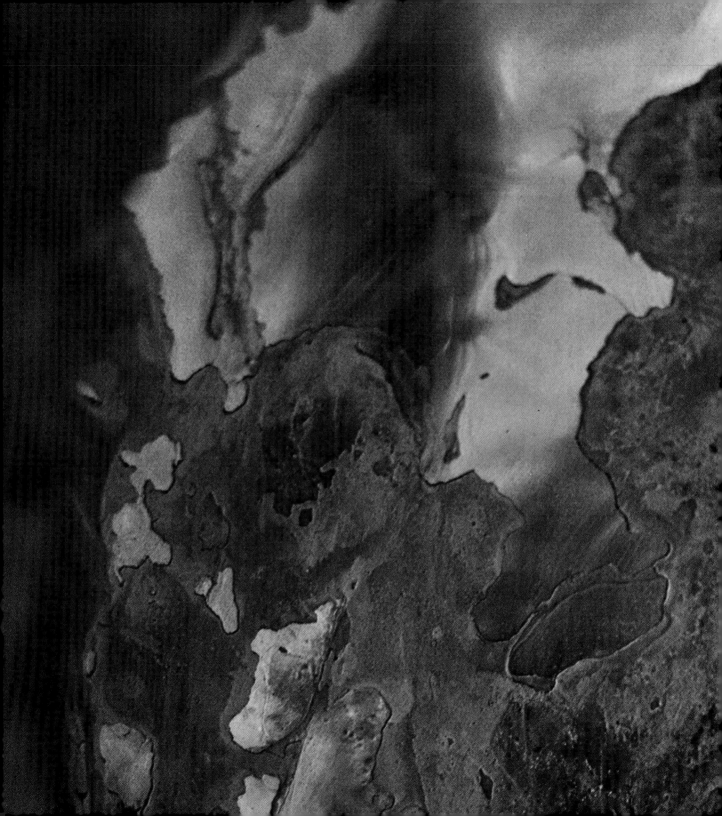

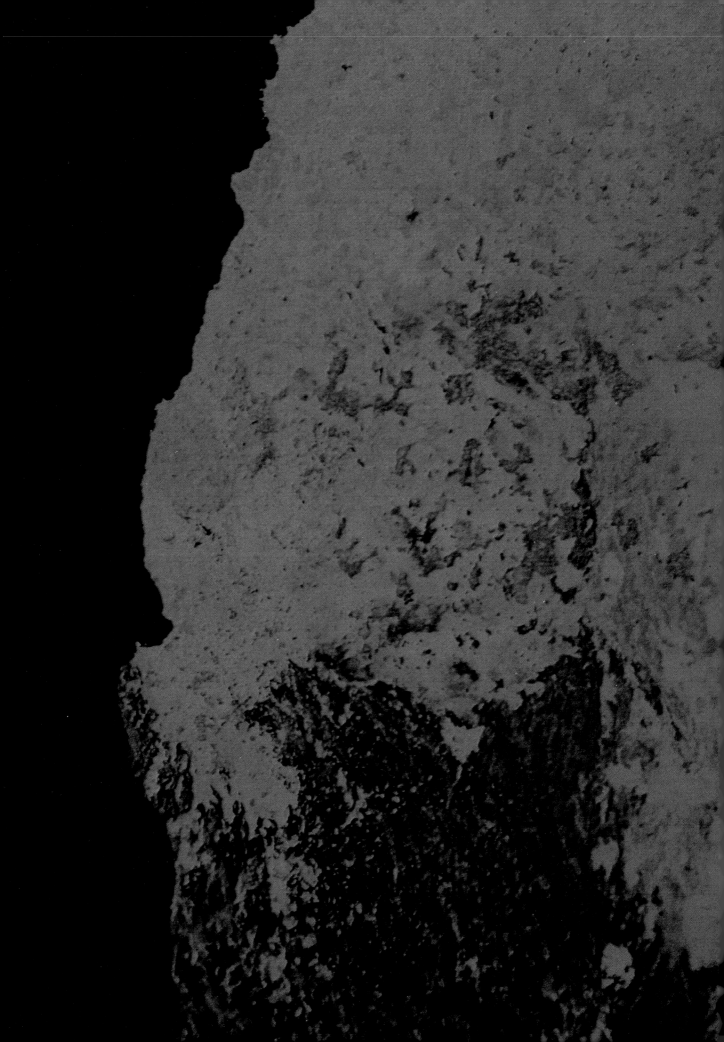

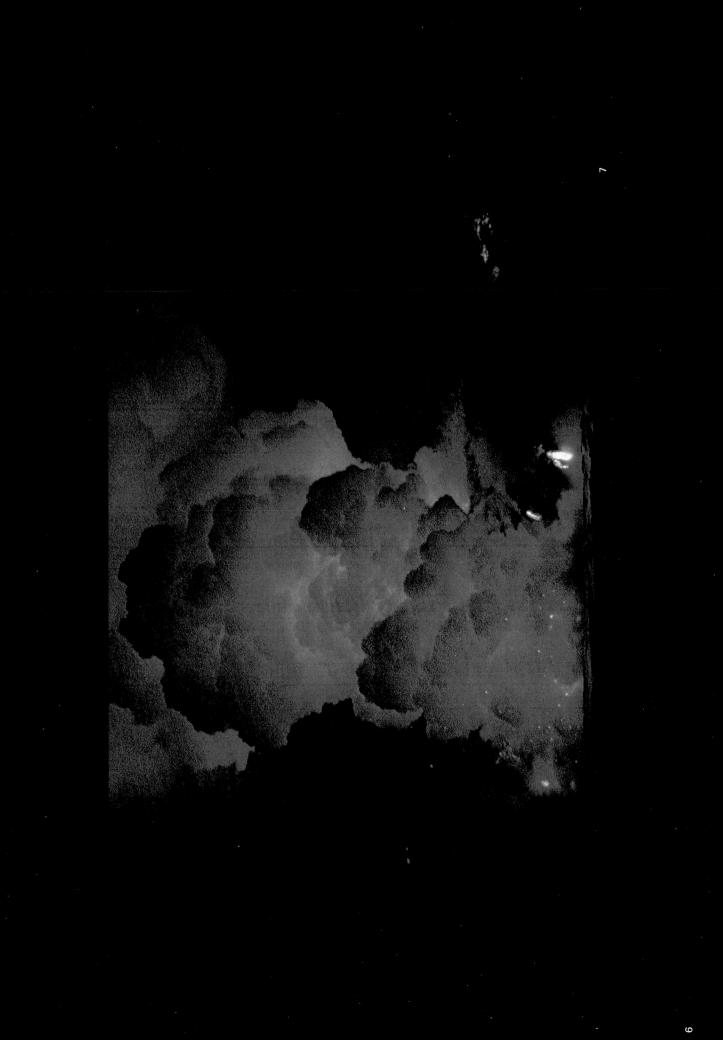

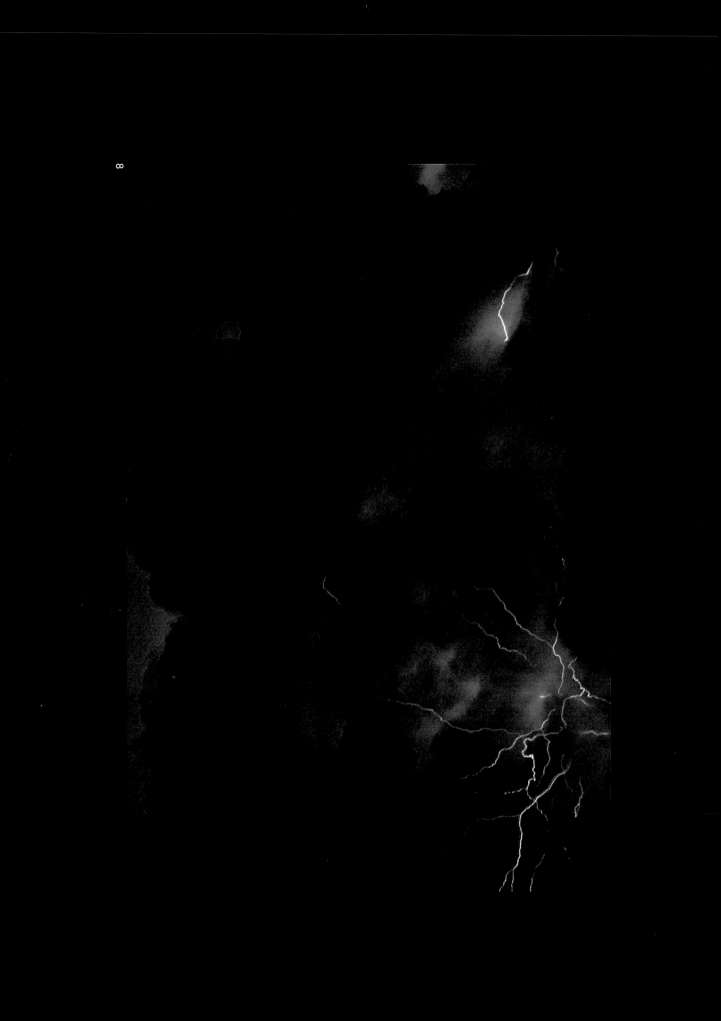

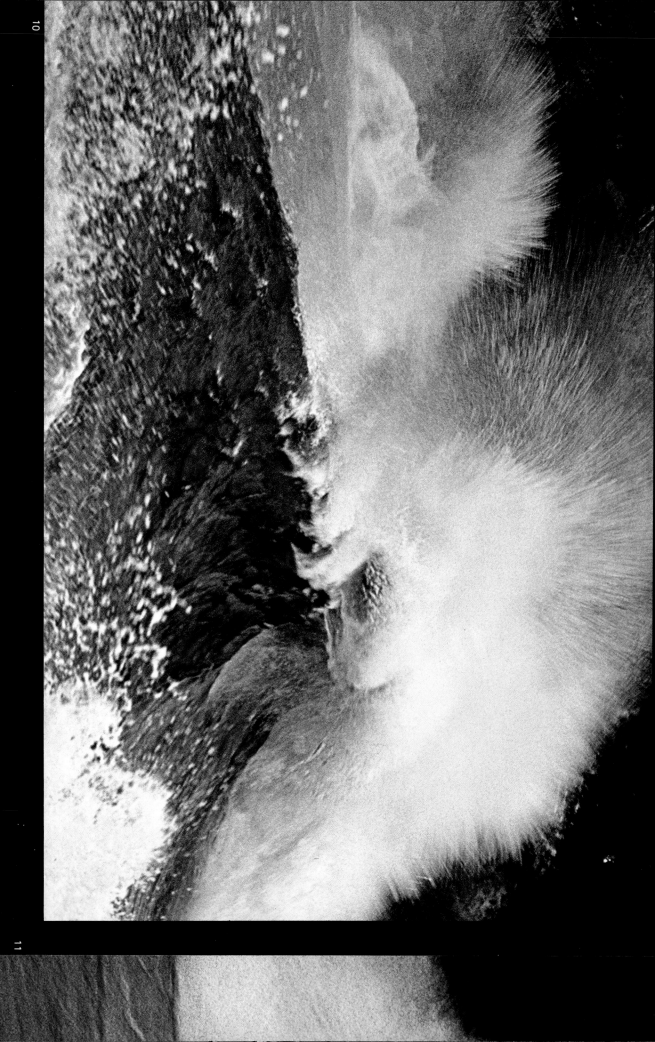

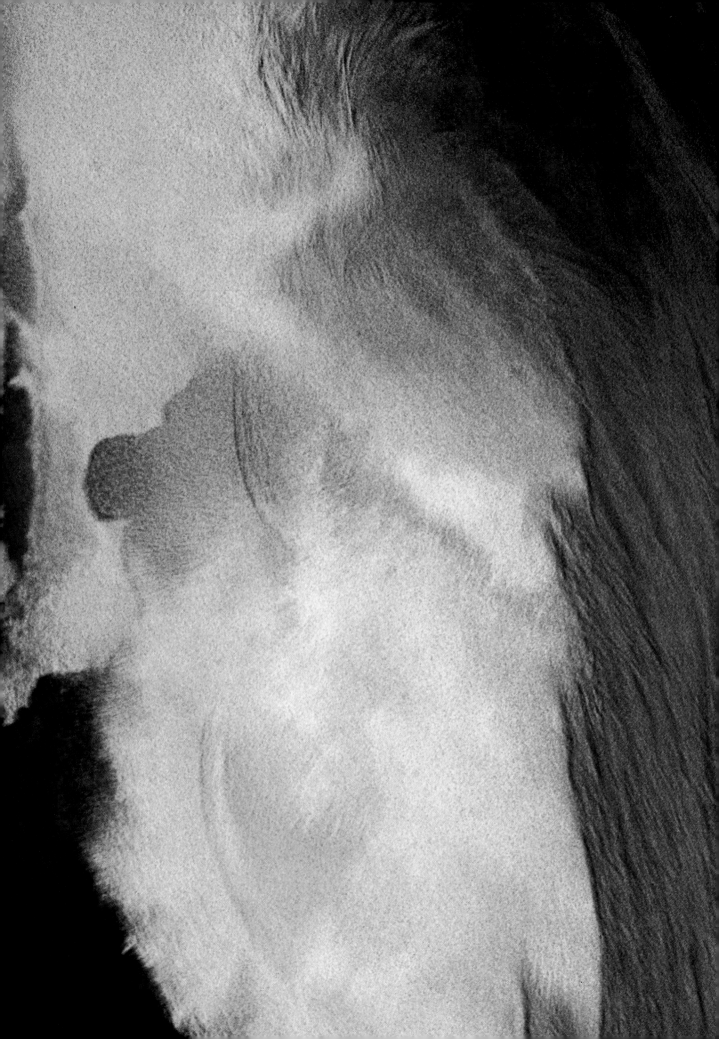

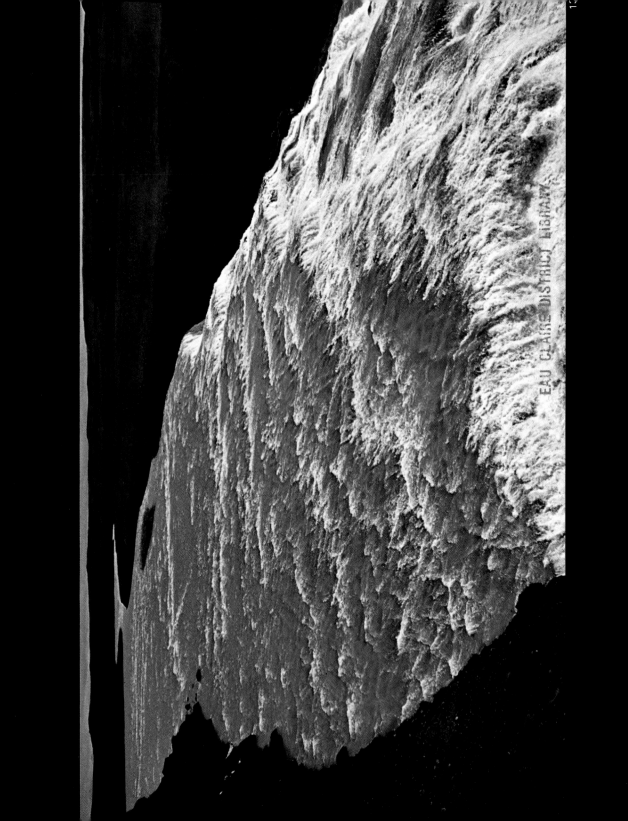

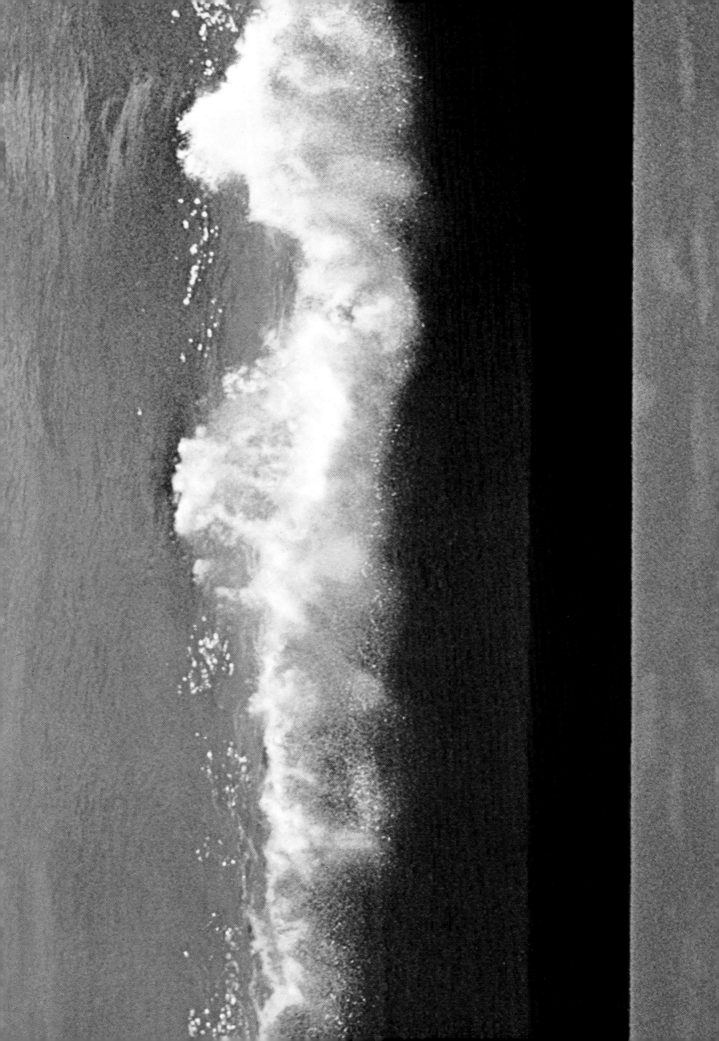

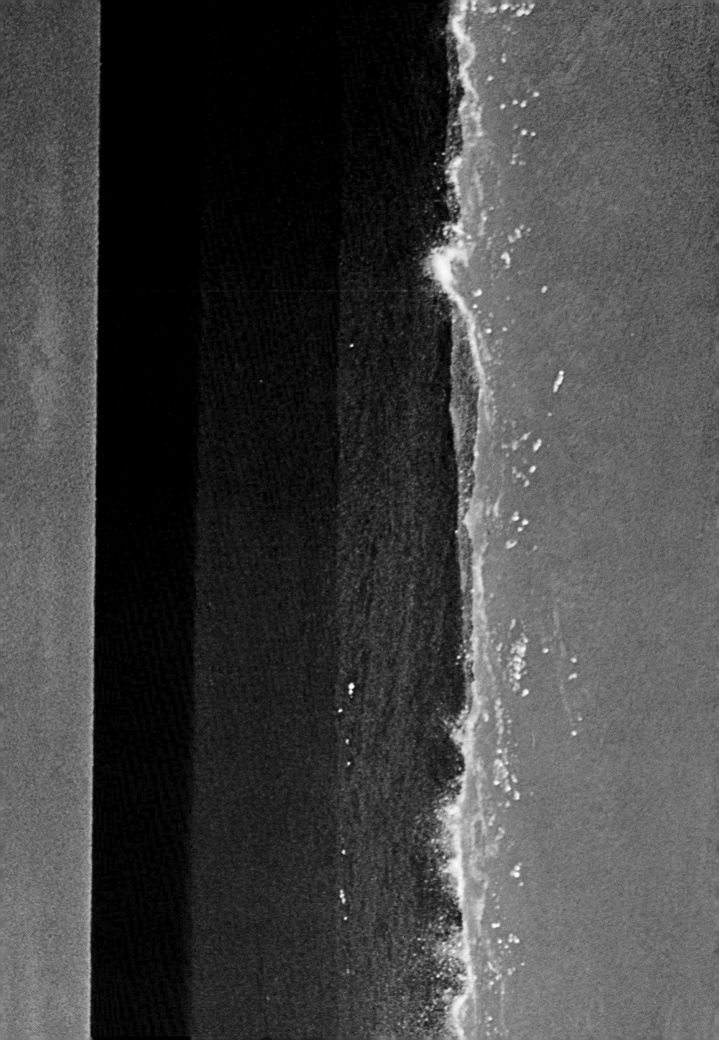

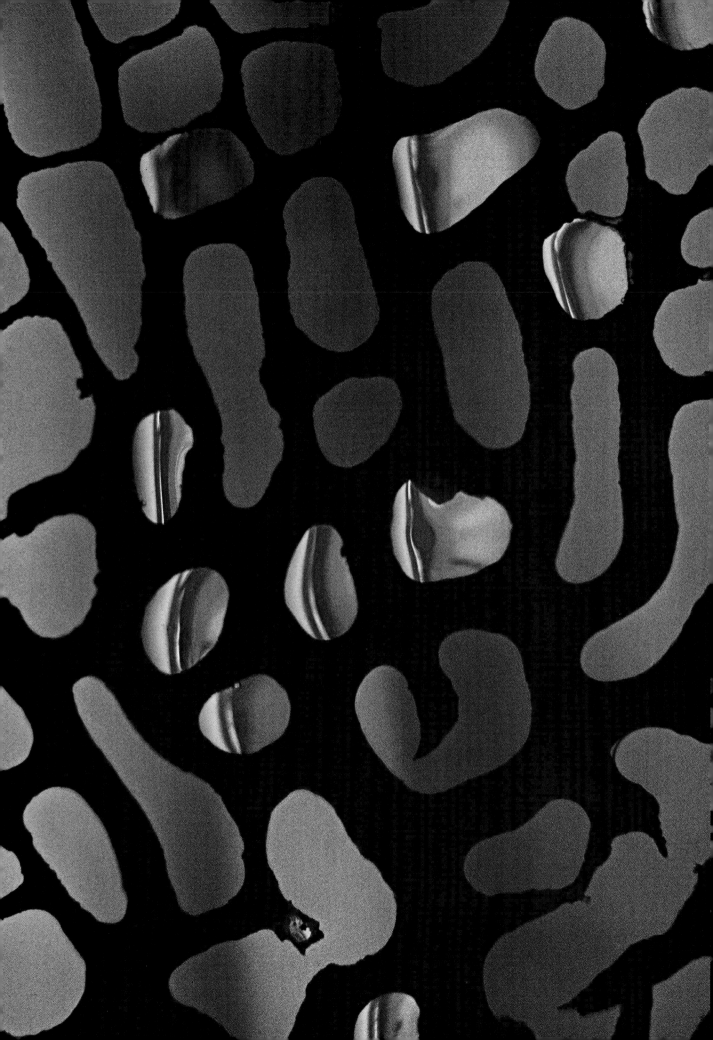

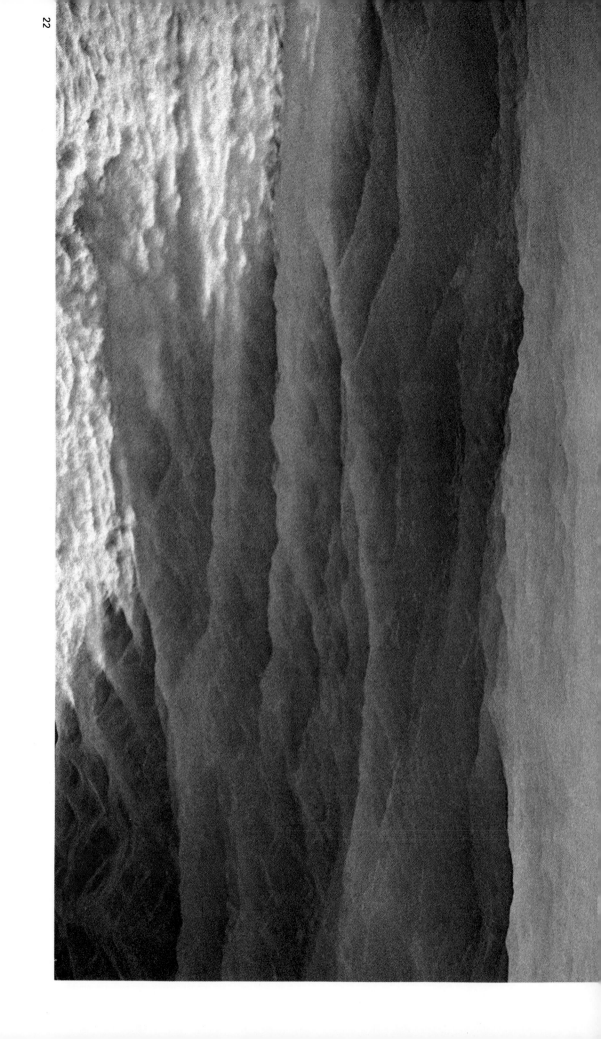

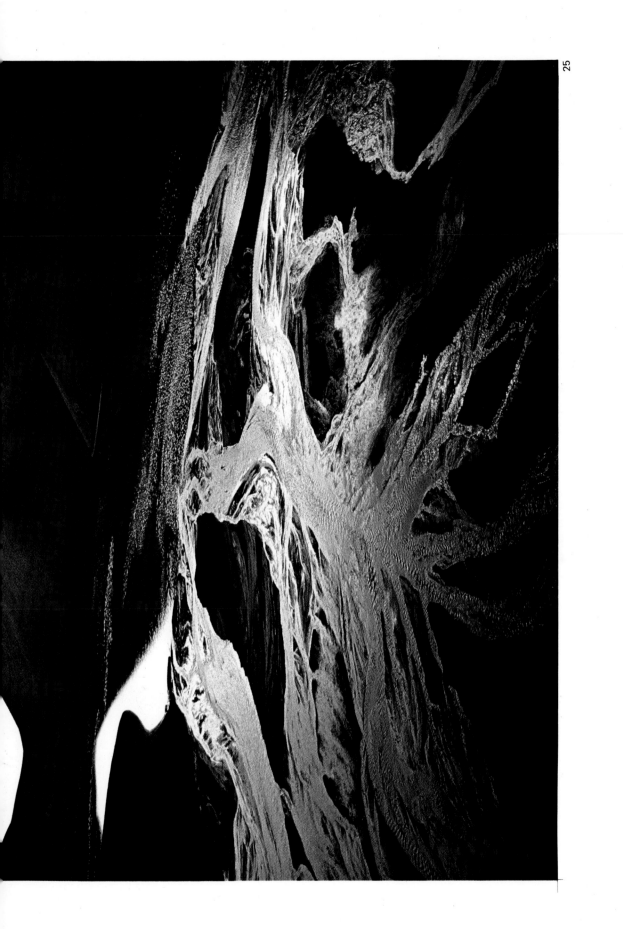

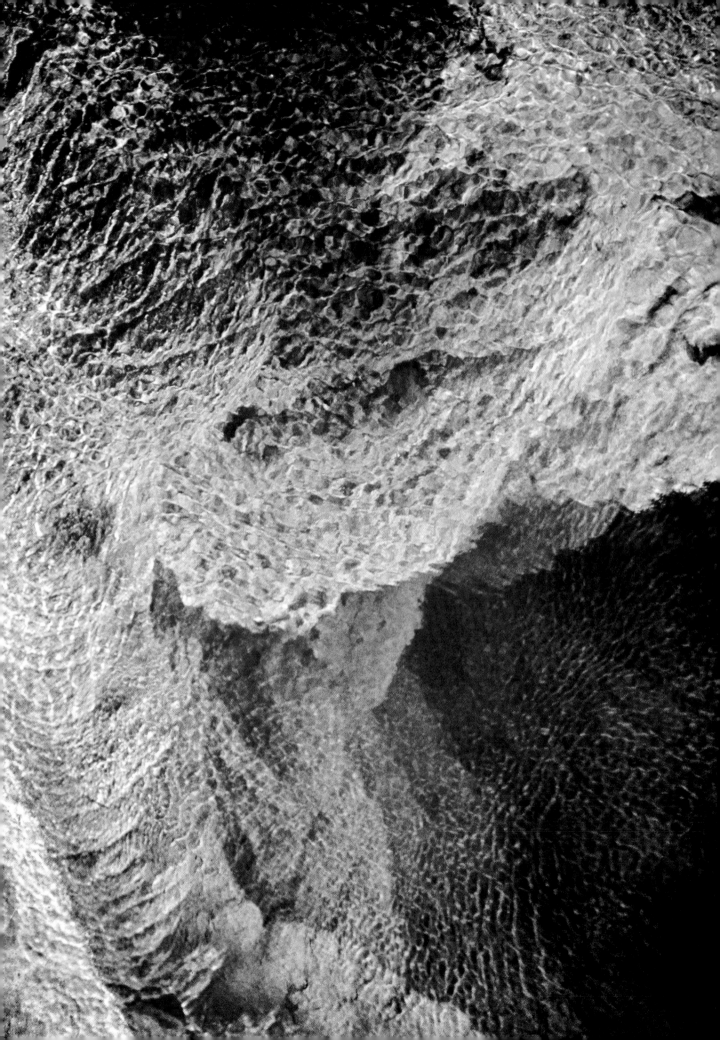

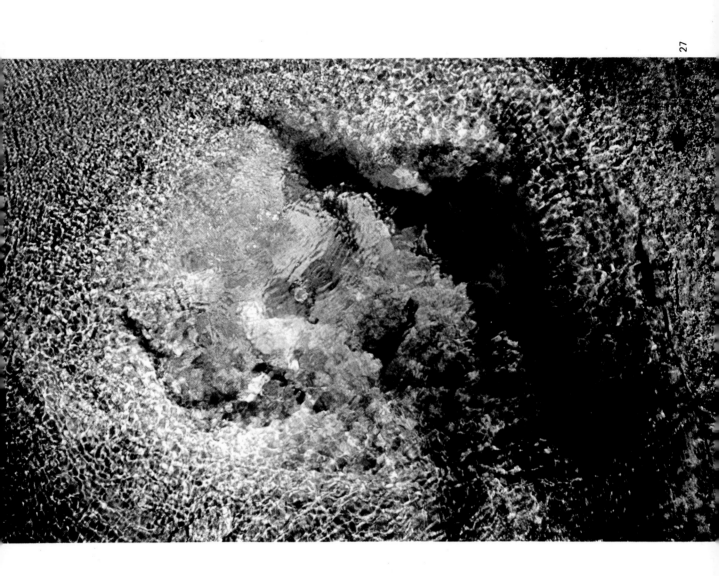

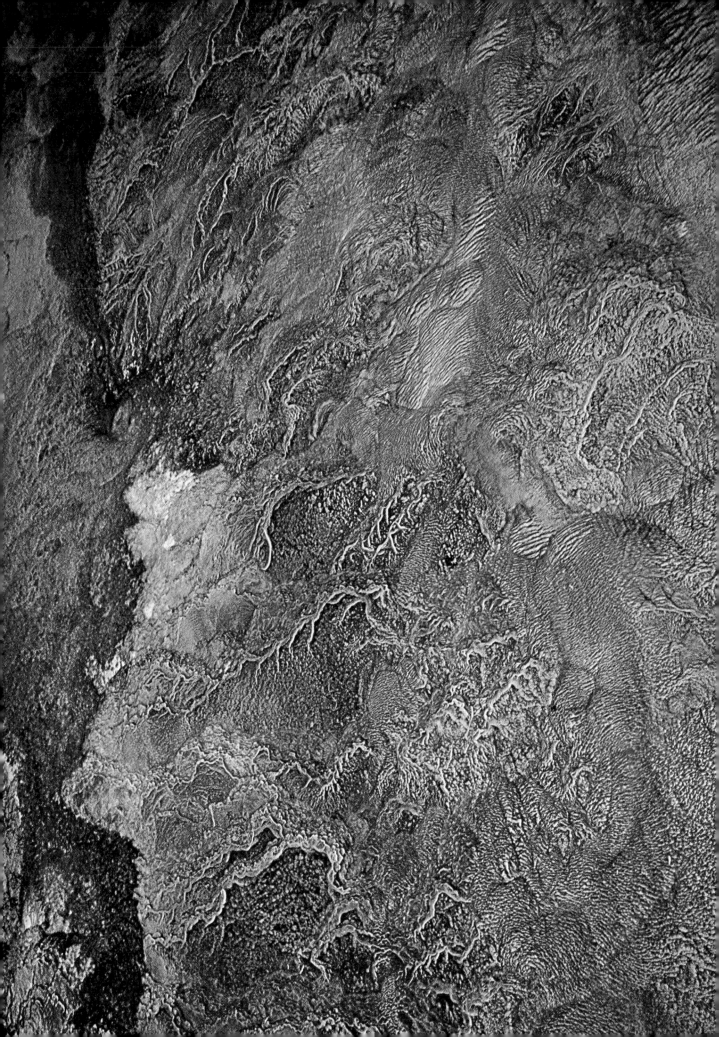

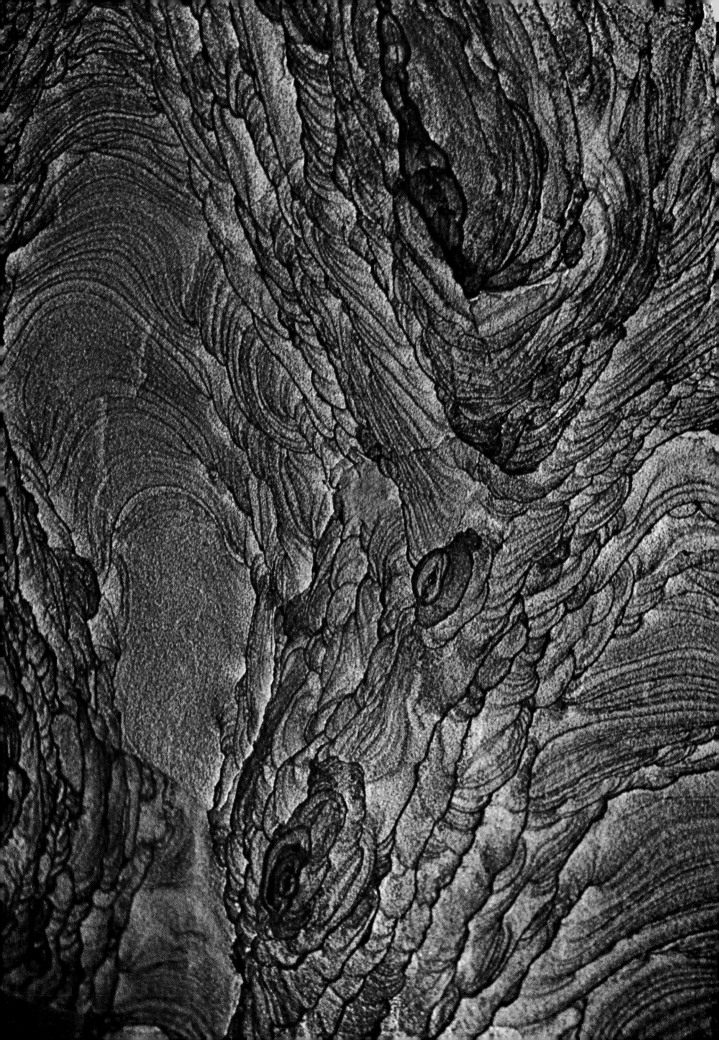

The Seasons

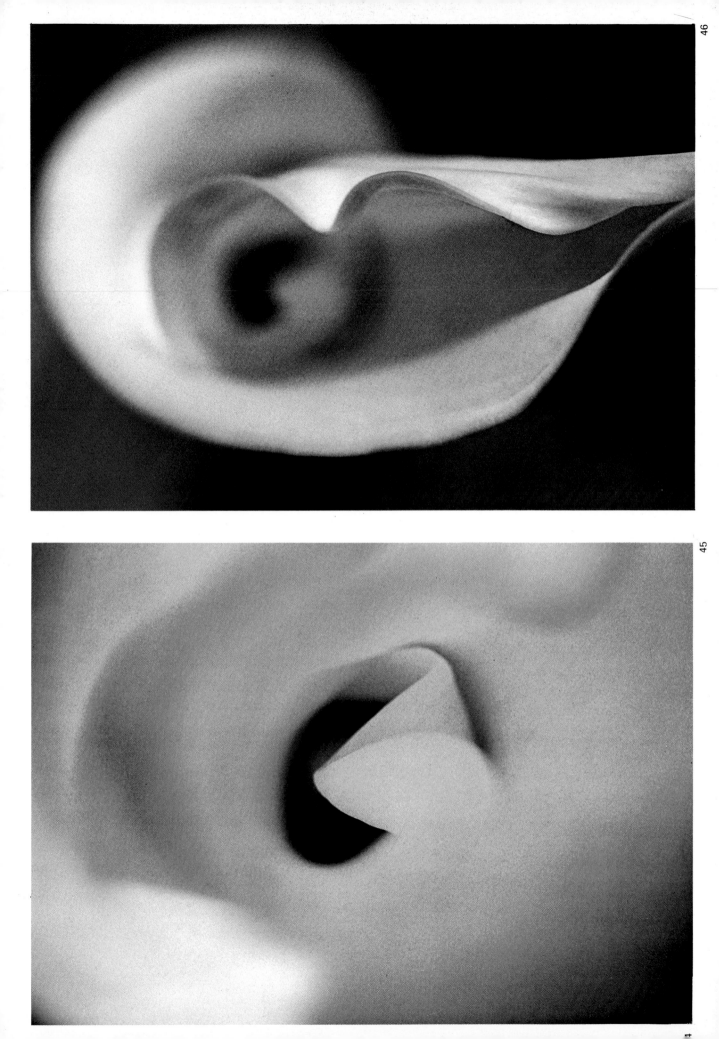

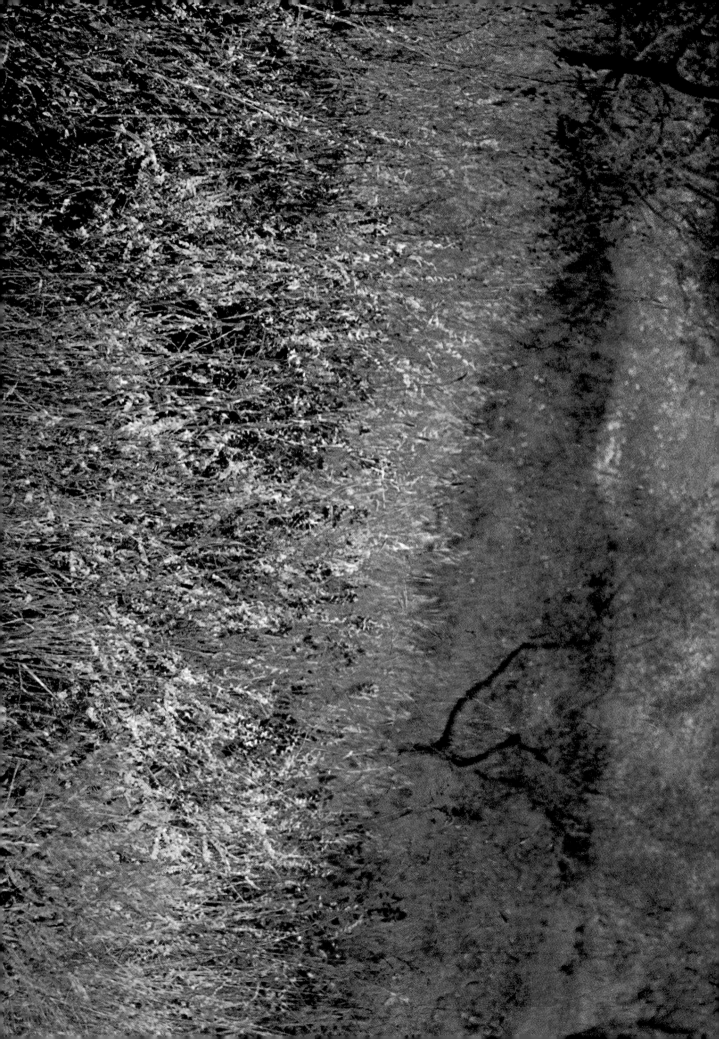

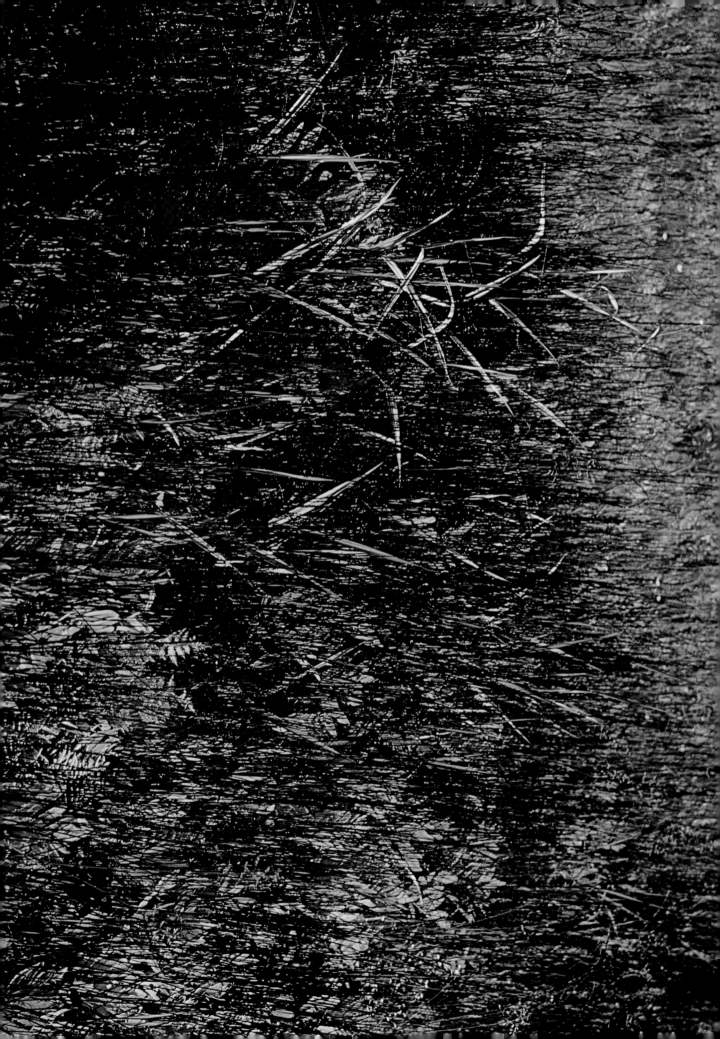

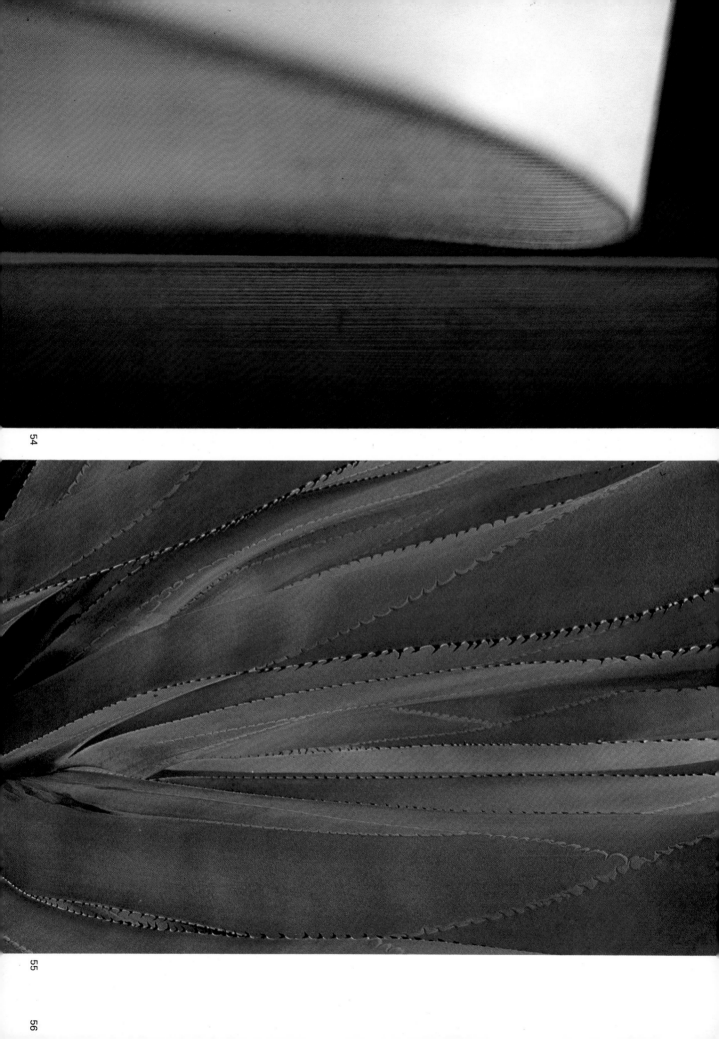

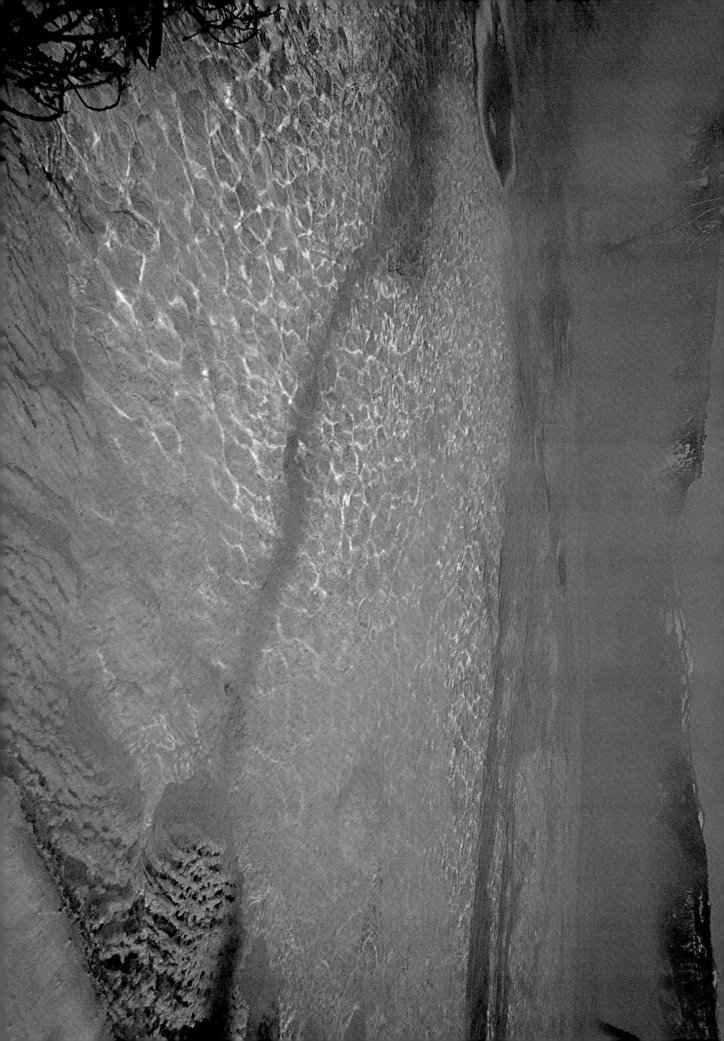

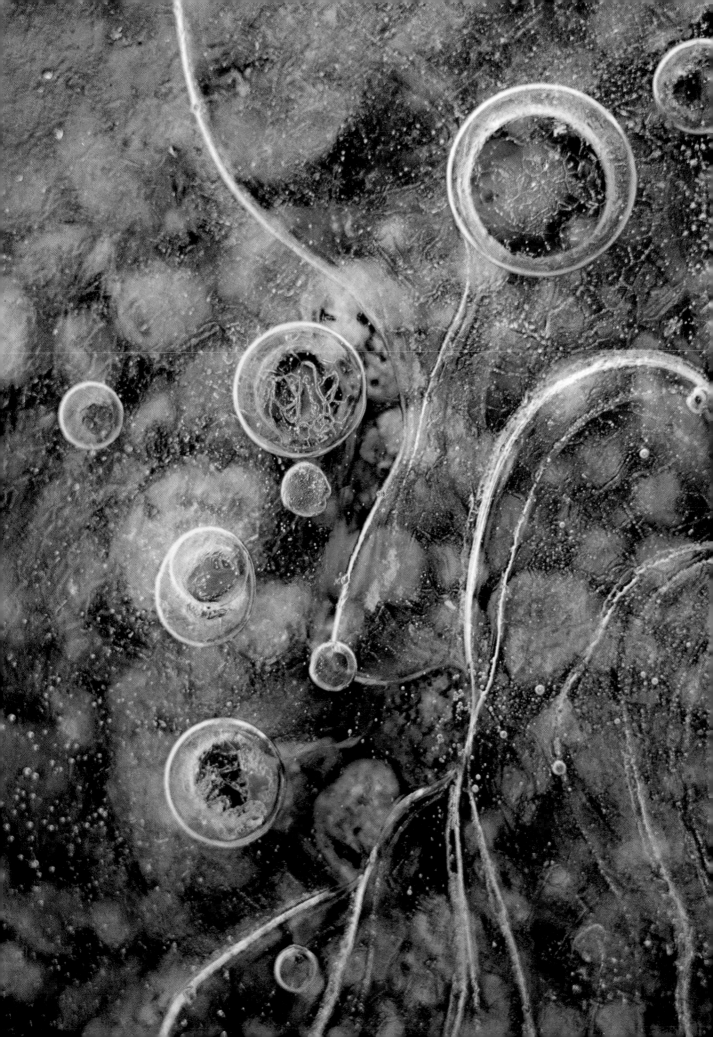

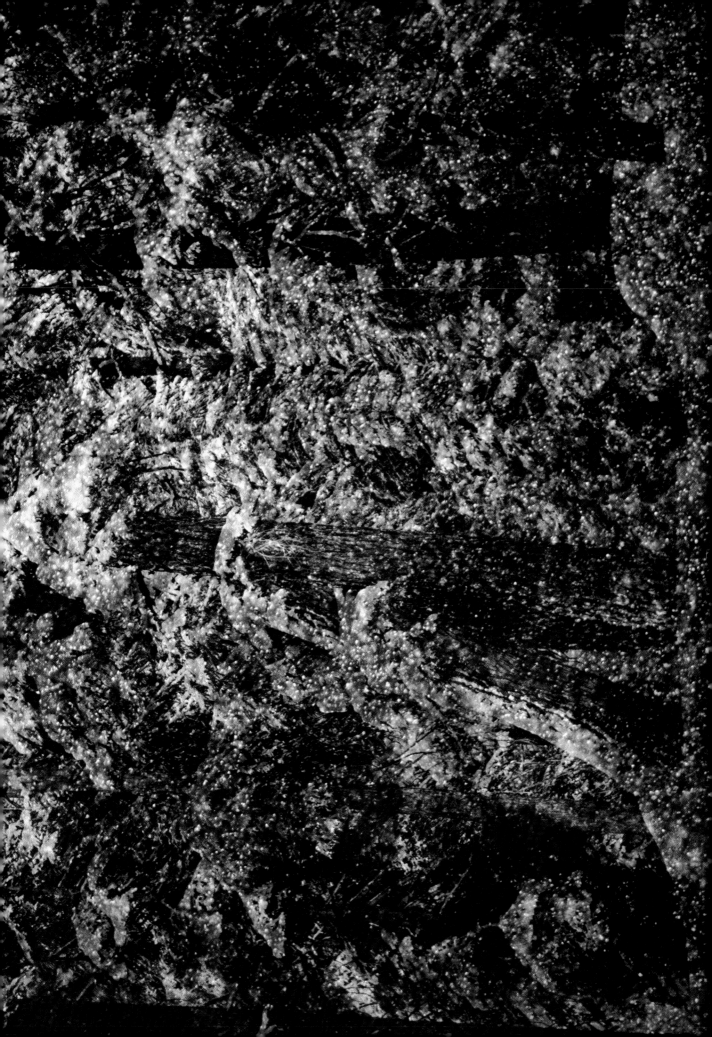

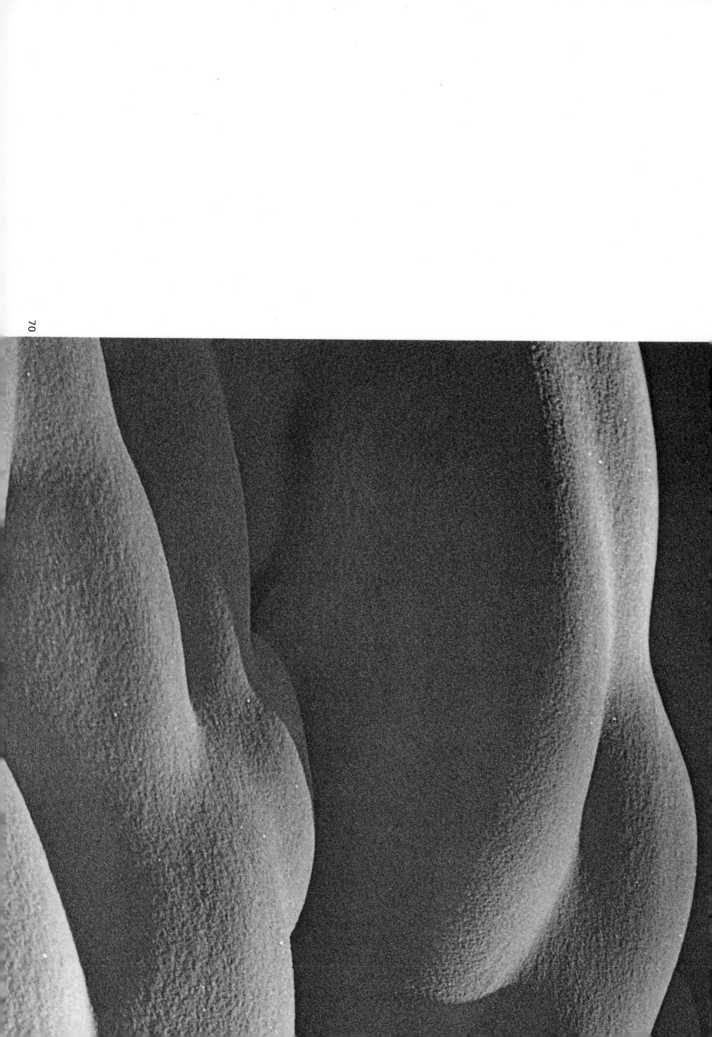

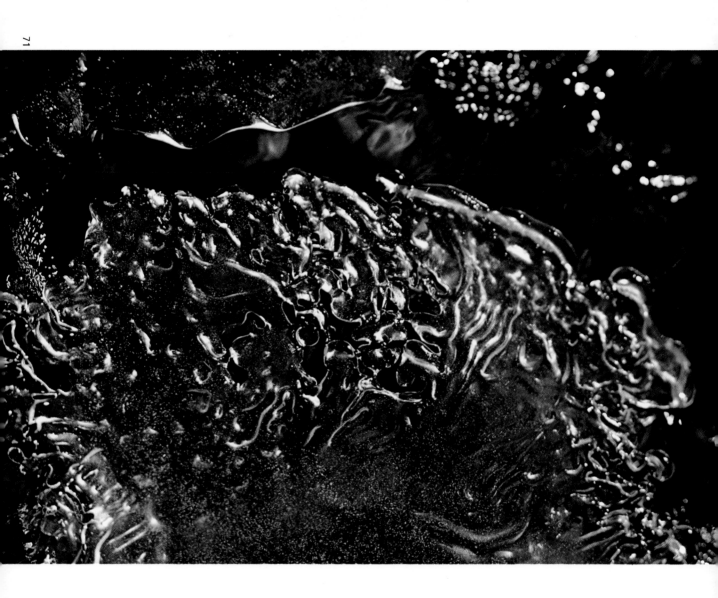

The Creatures

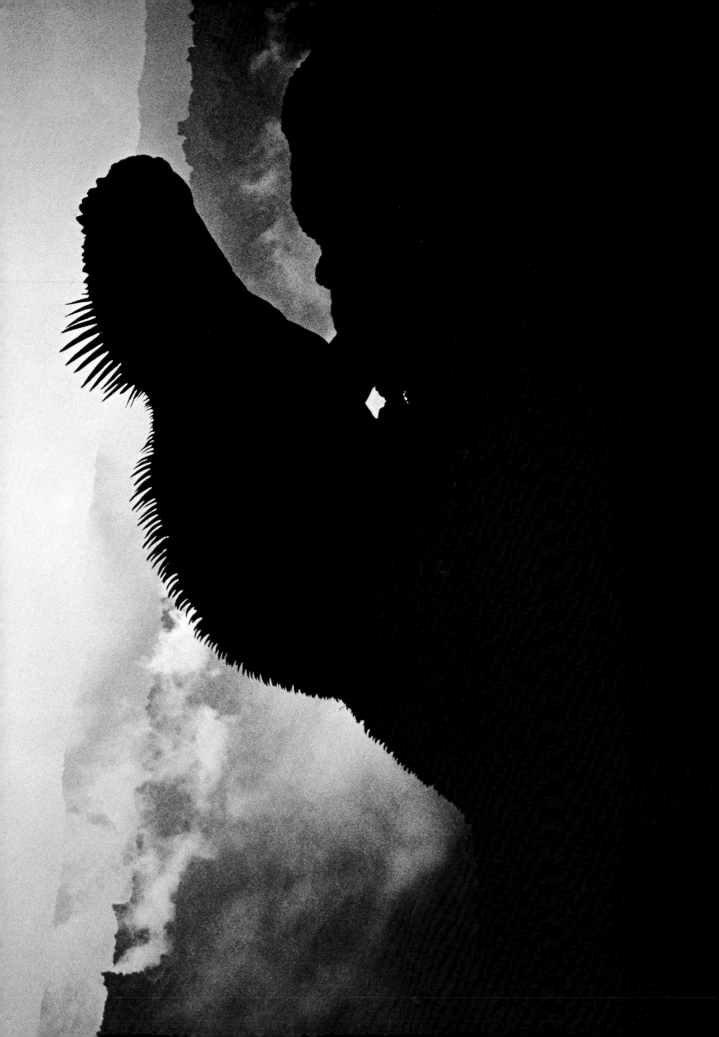

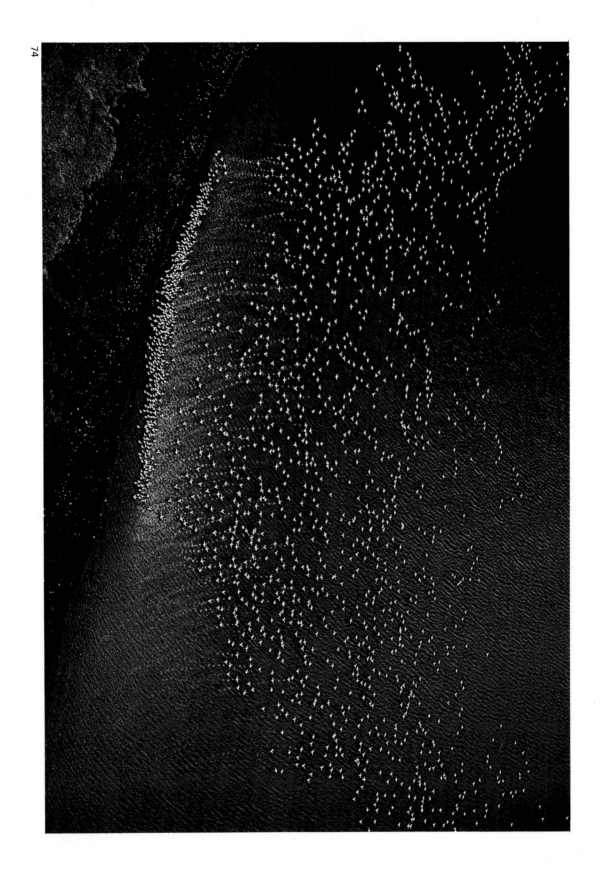

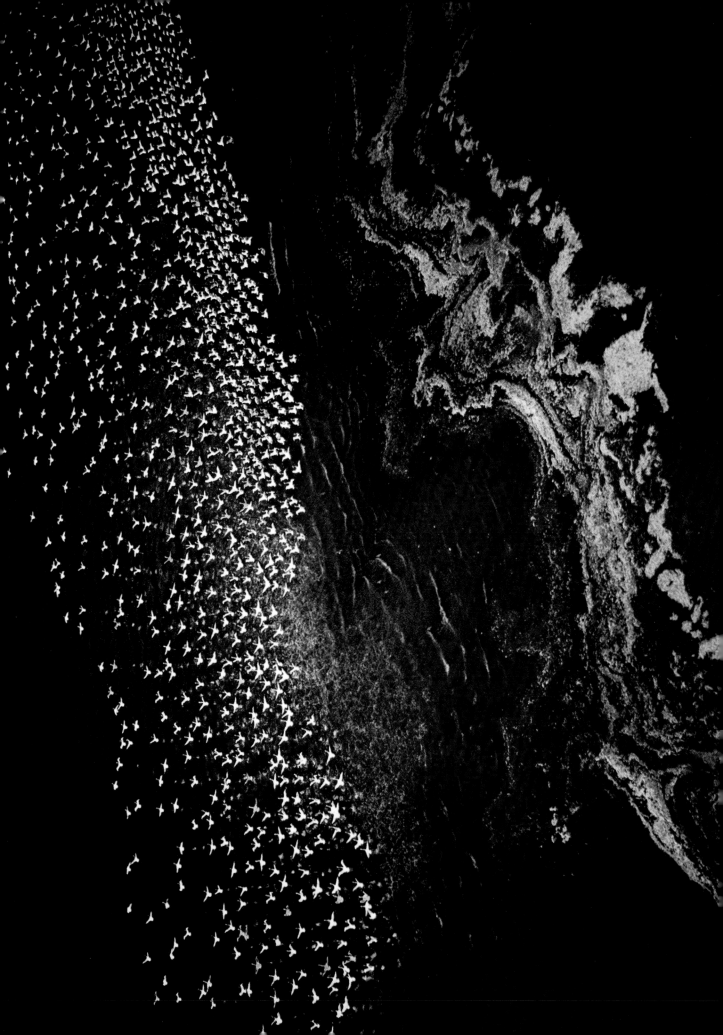

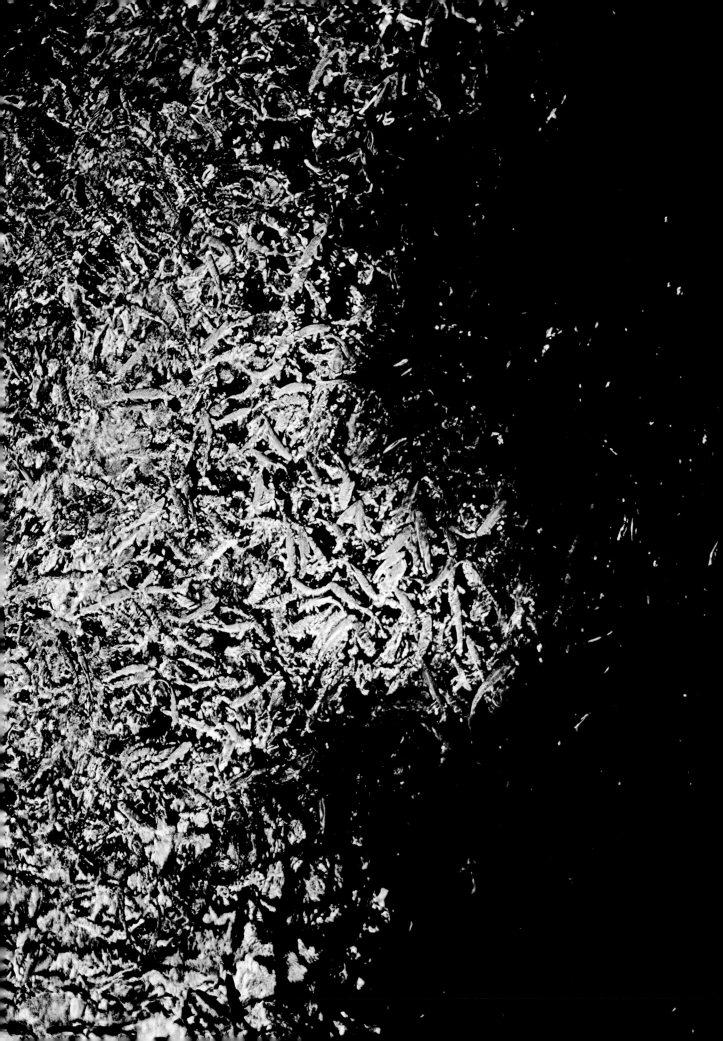

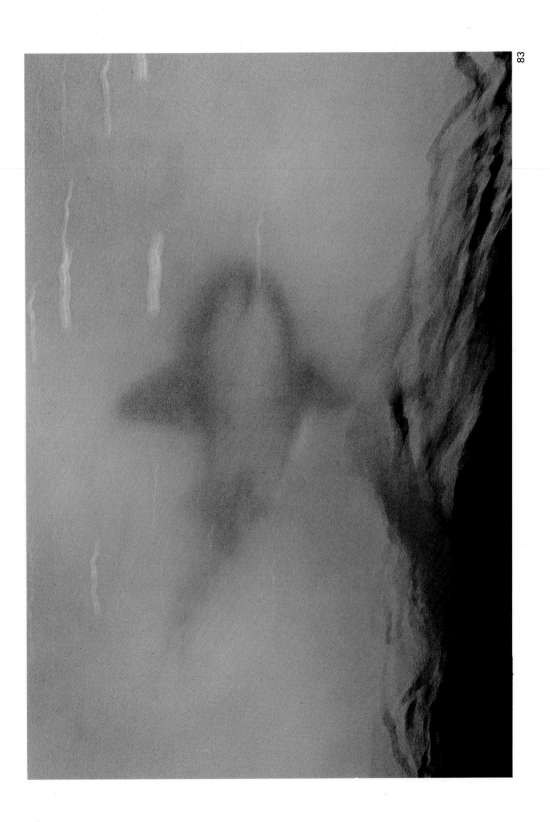

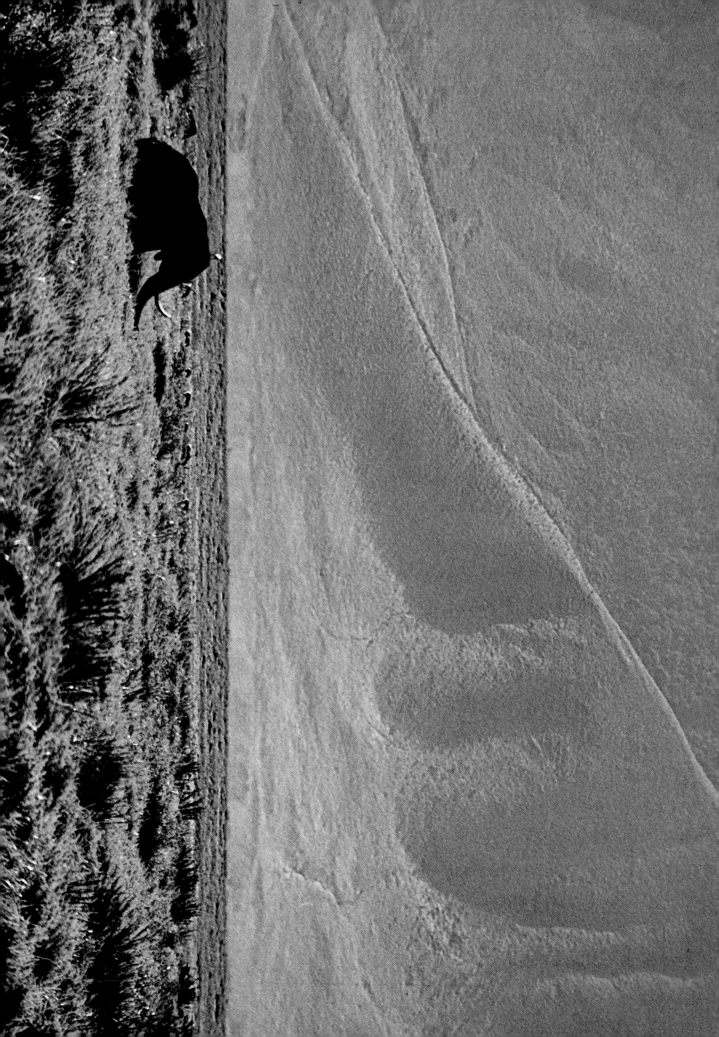

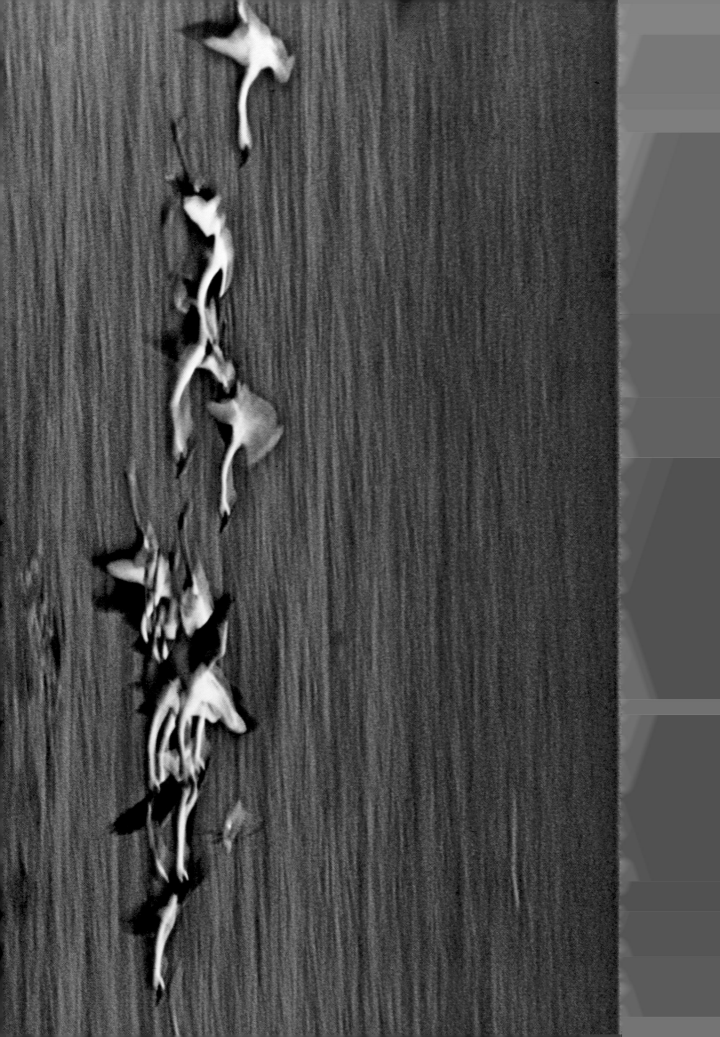

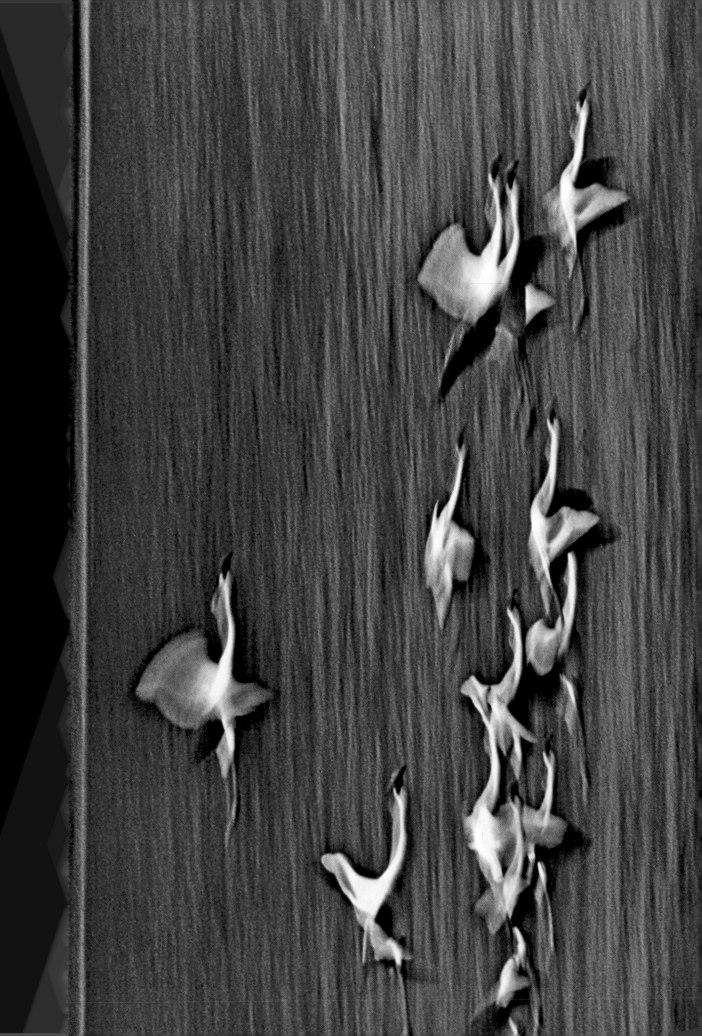

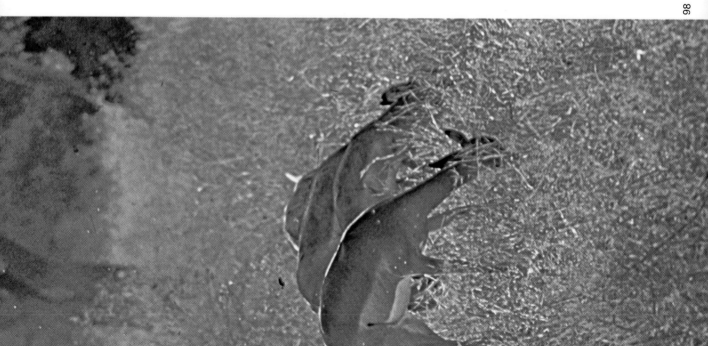

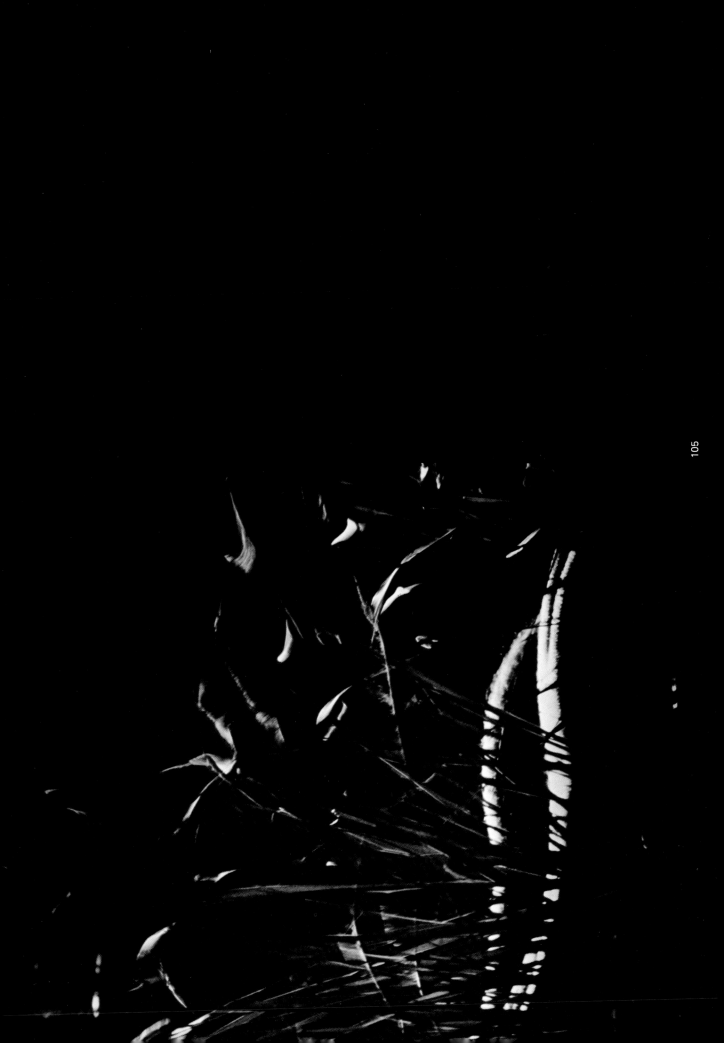

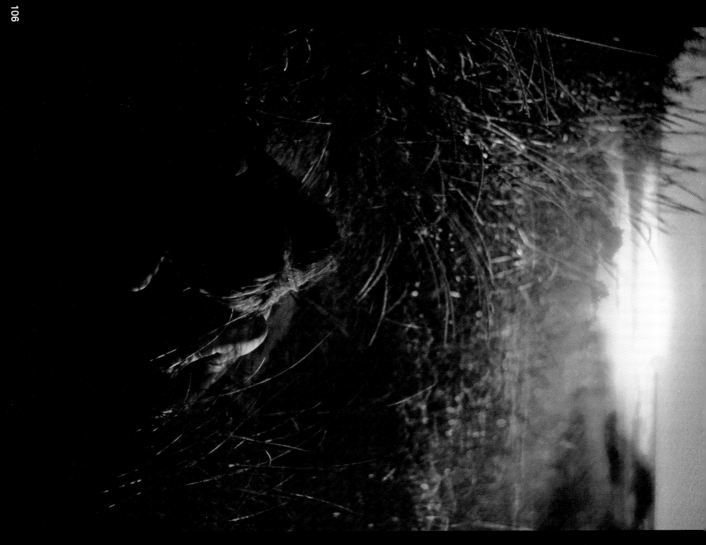

Many people who saw this collection of photographs prior to the publication of the book have asked how the theme developed in my mind and how I actually took the photographs.

In fact, the book evolved gradually. Perhaps the roots of it go back to the day I was born; certainly they lie in my early concern and fascination with natural history. But then, in 1959, I had an assignment with an industrial company which obliged me to think of dramatic ways in which to represent elemental power in photographic terms. I thought about the subject of power; I thought about the elements—air, water, fire, the earth. I also found myself thinking about sulphur, for, according to a text I had once read about alchemy, sulphur was once considered to be the fifth element. I went and viewed the sulphur pits in Yellowstone National Park, where the natural formations of sulphur reveal fantastic forms and textures. I took many photographs there, and in California; when the best of these were enlarged I found the results quite staggering. This led me to make further and further experiments along similar lines and in different regions of the world. It was not long before this new collection of photographs numbered in the thousands. I sorted them out and catalogued them in my library

under such headings as "air," "fire," "water," "minerals," "vegetation," ready for future use.

At this time it so happened that I had an assistant by the name—believe it or not—of Michelangelo. And one day when I came back to the studio after a long assignment he had assembled a number of my photographs in the projector. With a sparkle in his eyes, Michelangelo turned on some music. It was Haydn's music. Then, as he started to project the photographs, Michelangelo said to me, "Do you realize what you have photographed? You have photographed the creation of the world."

I continued to refine the collection and to round it out with new photographs. This process lasted until the end of 1970. Finally it was a question of dovetailing the pictures and making convincing sequences to symbolize the elements, the earth, the seasons, in fact, to symbolize the whole story of the Creation, as shown on the preceding pages.

For those readers who may be interested in how the pictures were taken, I have included a few brief notes about my equipment. These are followed by specific notes about the plates, the number being keyed to the numbers which appear next to the photographs (plates 1–106) in the illustrated section of the book.

Within the last ten years my camera equipment has changed somewhat, and so has the speed of color film. I have always used Kodachrome, and as testimony to its quality, I must say that even the photographs I took with the old film, Kodachrome I, have retained their color intensity through the years.

Since Kodachrome II came on the market I have used this newer film constantly. Because it has fine definition and almost no grain, I have never seen any reason to try out other materials. I don't mean this to sound like a plug for the film; I have never worked for Kodak—only *with* Kodak, and in so many different situations, that by now I know the film's characteristics by heart.

I am often asked if I use a tripod. I almost never do. I have to carry cameras, and because I like to travel light, I keep my equipment to a minimum. I have always worked with Leica M3 and M4 cameras and occasionally with Pentax cameras with Leica lenses attached. The Micro-Nikkor 55-mm. lens I find extremely useful for close-ups.

In the following notes, pictures that bear the dates 1969 to 1970 were taken with the new Leicaflex camera and lenses, which I find eminently satisfactory.

A final word about lenses and filters. I work mostly with lenses of 21, 28, 50, 90, 180, and 400 mm. I seldom use a filter, except for a polarization filter, which I find essential when I wish to reduce reflections and glare and also when taking photographs through the window of a plane or an automobile, which, for one thing, is never completely clean, and, for another, will usually pick up unwanted reflections from behind.

It is not my purpose to make this a technical treatise, and I assume that readers interested in learning what lenses to use for what occasions and, in general, how to handle a camera, color film, exposure meters, and other equipment, will turn to the many excellent technical books on the market or to the literature that the various manufacturers supply.

If I have any word of advice to give, it is that a photographer should learn to work with the minimum amount of equipment. The more you are able to forget your equipment, the more time you have to concentrate on the subject and on the composition. The camera should become an extension of your eye, nothing else.

The Elements

1. "God created the heaven and the earth. And the earth was without form and void." It was difficult to find an appropriate photograph for the opening plate of this book, but I kept returning to this one, which to me has a very special quality of light, space, and purity of color. I have always called it "Blue Light." It was made at dawn, shortly after a thunderstorm, while I was in a plane flying at an altitude of about twenty thousand feet over the Amazon.

2. Many years ago, while engaged on a missile story for a series of advertisements, I tried to find ways of symbolizing the power of the universe through the normal use of my 35-mm. camera. This picture, a result of one of my experiments, is a portion of an abalone shell, a reflection on the surface of a small sphere which suggests a vista of immense proportions. To me it also represents motion and changing light. I still own the shell and have tried many times to repeat and to improve on this shot, but as yet have never succeeded in rediscovering the angle and light that produced these particular reflections. The reason, of course, is that the surface of mother-of-pearl produces an infinite number of variations in color and shape. Looking into the shell gives almost as much to the eyes as a conch shell gives to the ear with the emulated sounds of the ocean. (1959)

3. A section of another abalone shell. The surface is concave, but the reflections it picked up make it appear convex,

suggesting the formation of a crust over the molten earth. As in plate 2, this is a straight shot taken with a Micro-Nikkor 55-mm. lens outdoors by available light. It was made at sunset, which gives it the reddish glow. (1970)

4 and 5. While I was working on John Huston's film *The Bible*, my most exciting venture was at Surtsey, near Iceland, the year the island was born. These pictures of the crater brewing and boiling at a fantastic temperature were taken around sunset, when there was just enough light to show the background color and just enough darkness to bring out the red heat of the lava flow. (1965)

6 and 7. At Surtsey a crew of us camped for four days on what was considered to be the safest site. It was as if we were watching a very fast and small-scale creation of the world. The huge crater kept erupting at irregular intervals and in different intensities. We rested in sleeping bags on very warm ground, changing our positions frequently to keep from getting too hot. In the early morning the earth was still steaming from the lava of the previous night's eruption, which flowed down into the ocean. (1965)

8. One night when I was in Khajuraho, India, an incredible thunderstorm developed, miles away, around midnight. I set my camera (equipped with a telephoto lens) on a tripod and then, leaving the aperture open, simply let the lightning serve as a flash. I didn't know what had been recorded until after the film was developed. (1968)

9. The impressive sight of ice and snow high up in the mountains of the Yosemite suggested to me a way of representing the image of a supercolossal storm. The photograph, used horizontally here, was actually shot vertically. I often photograph one subject with the purpose of emulating another, remaining, however, within the same element or a closely related one. It is then a question of composition and scale, which may involve the enlargement of some detail, or what movie people call false perspective. (1960)

10 and 11. Two more photographs taken at Surtsey. Our only real fear on this volcanic island was bad weather, which could cut us off from the mainland in the event of a sudden eruption. Luckily the storm shown in these views developed after we had boarded our boat. The islands seen in the background of plate 11 must have been created in much the same way as Surtsey. The force of huge, pounding waves, the raging wind, the heavy rain, and the strange quality of lava-formed rocks gave me the strongest feeling of the elements and of chaos that I have ever experienced. (1965)

12 and 13. At Gullfoss Falls, Iceland, in a landscape that is still untouched by man, the water pours over the falls in a powerful stream. Plate 12 is used to symbolize "Let there be a firmament in the midst of the waters, and let it divide the waters from the waters," and plate 13, "Let the dry land appear." The same kind of mood prevails on stormy days along almost any craggy coast where the rocks are washed by big waves that create innumerable waterfalls as the water recedes

- 150 -

and the surface of rock reappears. At Gullfoss it was easy to imagine a big flood surging over valleys and mountains, then gradually subsiding and leaving behind it a stream on the dry land. Plate 12 is a sandwich photograph: a duplicate transparency placed in reverse over the original one to produce the effect of divided waters. (1965)

14 and 15. "Let there be light." The first picture was photographed through the window of an airplane while it was flying through thick clouds during a thunderstorm in the Caribbean in 1970. The second one was taken in Norway from the deck of a boat during an early-morning fjord tour. I saw in this rare sight a perfect combination of the four elements—fire (represented by the sun), air, water, and earth. The scene expressed a unity I have never quite found again in this purely visual form. (1966)

16. This picture, which suggests the curve of the earth's surface, might from the look of it have been shot from way out in space, but in fact it is the result of false perspective. The lava ashes of the Surtsey volcano form a mountain-like dome of such immensity and sharp, smooth outline that, whenever the sun rises or sets over its horizon, it is easy to imagine that one is viewing the earth from a tremendous distance. Wind and rain must have formed the smooth surface of this mound of ashes so unlike that of an ordinary mountain. (1965)

17 and 18. "And God . . . divided the waters which *were* above the under the firmament from the waters which *were* above the

firmament. . . ." To represent this difficult passage in Genesis, the best solution I could find was a symbolic interpretation showing a rainbow over the sea. Taking the photograph for plate 17 proved to be quite a traumatic experience, for the small plane in which I was flying over Miami (in 1963) was sucked up by clouds and went much higher than the pilot intended it to go. The pilot, a young photographer embarking on his first solo flight, invited me along. Not understanding much about aeronautical problems, I became overenthusiastic about the perspectives he was revealing to me and I begged him not to fly higher. It hadn't occurred to me that he was unable, just then, to do anything but keep on going up, up, and up! There were two rainbows, a phenomenon I had never seen. The second rainbow in plate 17 is hardly visible in the photograph, because at this point we had suddenly started a perilous descent. What is seen is all that I managed to capture on film. The second time I photographed a double rainbow was in Iceland two years later. This is shown in plate 18. (1965)

19. Along the coast of Tobago, when the sun had begun to reappear following a thunderstorm. The shifting clouds threw shadows on the ocean, creating many different shades of green and blue. This beautiful sight is particularly Caribbean. I used a 180-mm. Sonnar lens and an exposure of 1/500 second at f.2. (1968)

20. The smooth, rippling water of a fjord touched by the glancing shadow of a mountain. The colors and patterns re-

flected in the surfaces of lakes and rivers provide almost endless variations for photographic studies. (1966)

21. Water left in the crevasses of a coral after it had been washed by a wave. Small isolated puddles make a mosaic of the beach and sky in several magnified long-distance reflections. (1963)

22. This picture, made from a plane shortly after take-off from California, represents something of a paradox. The almost wavelike fluidity of the mountains, which, I imagine, might have looked like this in the very beginning of the world, is in fact very modern smog shrouding the mountains around Los Angeles. (1962)

23. During movie-making, when locations are off the beaten track and long periods of waiting occur between takes, I have always used the opportunity to build up my collection of photographs of natural phenomena. Here at Mazatlán, Mexico, while I was working on *Kings of the Sun*, the sea was very close to the set. As I sat watching the waves roll in, my attention kept returning to the strange formations in the sand, which constantly changed with the movement of the very shallow, gentle waves. Through the use of a wide-angle lens, and a polarizing filter to eliminate reflections, I created a landscape which can assume any dimension the eye or mind might wish to give to it. (1963)

24. Shortly after World War II, I first saw and was inspired

by the work of Edward Weston, although I tried in every possible way to avoid copying him. Many years later I found this water-covered rock on the beach at Point Lobos, California, where Weston lived and took many of his famous photographs. Big waves kept sending streams over the surface of the rock, abstracting the many colors of the sea fauna below it and fragmenting it into innumerable hues of ocher, green, and blue. To freeze the fast motion of the water I used a shutter speed of 1/1000 second at f.2. (1959)

25. The broad, glittering expanse of a lagoon on Surtsey, seen from the summit of the volcano at sunset. (1965)

26. Looking down into Hveravellir Geyser in Iceland, just as the geyser had begun to show signs of eruption by sending up bubbles. In between eruptions the beautiful blue water is extraordinarily still and clear, permitting one to peer down into its depths which harbor all kinds of mysterious images and reflections. (1965)

27. The still, coppery depths of another geyser, thousands of miles away, in Yellowstone National Park, Wyoming. (1960)

28 and 29. These pictures, which look like primeval landscapes with plants beginning to take form, are actually detail shots of the sulphur pits of Mammoth Hot Springs in Yellowstone National Park. Plate 29 shows a smaller detail, a section of the pit which is about three feet wide by five feet long, while the area shown in the second photograph covers

approximately a hundred square feet. For both studies I used a 21-mm. Leica wide-angle lens. (1961)

30 and 31. In Utah there is a certain kind of desert rock called "picture rock," eroded by sand, wind, and rain into fabulous patterns that give the illusion of a third dimension. In these photographs, taken at a quarry, one has the impression of looking into two fantastic caves. (1961)

32. Although this might appear to be a photograph of sand dunes, it is actually a detail shot of the wall of an Arizona sand cave, taken from an unusual angle. (1964)

33. A section of another picture rock, with a labyrinth of lines that suggest the images of a Madonna and Child. (1961)

34 and 35. Neither of these landscapes exists except in pictures. Millions of years ago the awesome formations were covered with water, and today they are back in their original state due to the building of the Glen Canyon Dam. I took the photographs in untouched lands along the Colorado River, the site chosen for the filming of *The Greatest Story Ever Told*. While waiting for the shooting to begin, I had days to wander through this fascinating territory right in the middle of the Navajo reservation. The earth, vast and dry, seemed to be waiting for a coming green. (1963)

36. Volcanic cones found in the Andes around Quito, Ecuador, overgrown with grass and ripe for richer vegetation.

One can imagine a rainbow initiating the first cycle of the seasons and the colors of flowers to come. (1965)

The Seasons

37. "Spring." An interpretation of the first of the seasons, photographed in Sicily. The impressionistic effect, intended to represent the essence of spring, was achieved through a double exposure. First I photographed the meadow out of focus and slightly overexposed; then I took exactly the same scene in focus on the same frame of film. The camera was hand-held for both exposures. (1965)

38 and 39. Details of wildflowers in a field. For both pictures I used a close-up lens to bring out the flowers' essential grace and beauty. (1967)

40. Showers are as characteristic of spring as warm sunshine. Here I wanted to emphasize the feeling of rain, so I used a slow shutter speed which enabled me to keep the pink blossoms in sharp focus while allowing the fast-falling raindrops to project themselves in long, wet streaks across the entire picture. (1970)

41. Masses of blossoms photographed from a hill in New York City's Central Park. Through one group of laden branches, others, and yet others on more distant trees contribute to the soft profusion of pink and white. (1970)

42 and 43. The miracle of creation is continually manifested by the cycle of plant life. These two studies show an early and late stage of an egglike bud evolving into a flower. I photographed the rose at intervals of a half-hour or so as it gradually opened into full bloom. The pictures were made indoors, using available light and my normal Micro-Nikkor 50-mm. lens. (1970)

44–46. Three more studies of flowers, made outdoors and with the use of a close-up lens. To get sharp detail I set the camera at f.8 and was obliged by the subdued light to use a low shutter speed of 1/10 second. I found a convenient piece of wood nearby, which I picked up and propped under my elbow to steady the camera in my hand. To accommodate a slow exposure (less than 1/25 second) I would always much rather use some handy prop like this than carry a tripod around. (1971)

47. "Summer." The warmth and color of the season is expressed in a double-exposure photograph, taken in the same manner as the interpretation of "Spring" seen in plate 37. (1964)

48. Looking across a valley in Italy, at a magic moment when the trees were tinged by the late-afternoon sun. The suggestion is of a river of gold flowing down through the hollow of the hills. (1964)

49. The middle of a forest. Another double exposure. For the

second take (on the same frame of film) shifting the camera slightly to the left resulted in a denser, fuller-looking woodland scene, which was the effect I was seeking. (1961)

50. Detail of a forest floor. The interesting groundcover pattern with a dominant shoot was photographed in midsummer. (1970)

51. A marshy spot in Dark Harbor, Maine, dense with grasses and weeds in various shades of green. I find nature's background color the most challenging of all to photograph, especially in summer, when the light greens of spring have turned much darker. (1965)

52. In the normal course of viewing nature, smaller images are often overlooked. When this highlight on a blade of grass caught my attention, I decided to make a close-up shot of it. By photographing the leaf against the evening sun, I was able to isolate and abstract the surface reflection with its several shades of green, leaving the rest of the blade in shadow. (1969)

53. A blade of wild grass curling in onto itself after the first chilly night of late summer. (1968)

54–56. Three studies representing different aspects and stages of growth. In plate 54, the thin red line (the edge of a cactus leaf) expresses upward growth; the bent leaf in the foreground, the beginning of decay. The second study, also of a cactus, reveals the cathedral-like inner structure of a plant. The third photograph, showing the leaves of a giant *Xanthosoma mataff* plant looming over a rain forest in Ecuador, symbolizes the end of time of growth, the flesh of the leaves having been eaten away by insects. Only a skeleton remains. Plates 54 and 55 were taken in 1969; plate 56, in 1965.

57. "Autumn." An unusual effect created by making two separate exposures of the same scene, each in normal focus but from different distances, on the same frame of film. Both shots were slightly underexposed, so that the two together take on the appearance of a single normally exposed photograph. Because the background and foreground of the wood were photographed separately, the colors melt into each other and produce a most effective composition. (1966)

58. In the Arizona desert, the subtle hues of the autumn landscape, the thorny bushes, the sandy rock, and even the sky seemed almost to be variations of the same color. In the far background what appears at first glance to be a cloudy sky is the surface of a rock. (1963)

59–61. Curling, drying leaves, photographed on a warm autumn day early in the morning. Dew helped heighten the color of the leaves, and in plate 61 the moisture in the air contributed to the rainbow-like reflection of the lightray breaking through the branches. (1969)

62 and 63. Two studies of the same leaf made early one misty

morning. In the first close-up, each raindrop is like a tiny magnifying glass, enlarging small sections of the leaf. In the second, longer-range picture, moisture from the leaf, absorbed by the wet stone, has created a dark natural frame around it. (1969)

64 and 65. Winter fantasy. As the Mammoth Hot Springs battle against the cold of winter, melting snow and ice around their edges create blankets of steam in the freezing air. Plate 65 shows mist rising over the sulphur pits. (1966)

66 and 67. Ice patterns. Through the almost frozen surface of a river, the rocks and stones lying at the bottom have assumed unusual shapes and colors. Plate 67 shows bubbles in a thin layer of ice covering a small stream. Both patterns seem to be reflections of the universe itself. (1966)

68 and 69. Two pictures which capture winter in its absolute. Accumulations of snow on the branches make the trees look as if they were covered with blossoms. Plate 69 is a double exposure. I trained my Leica on the trees, photographing them at 1/25 second; then I took a second shot on the same frame of film (at 1/100 second), focusing on the flakes near to the camera. (1966)

70. The inanimate often suggests the animate. Here, the smooth, flowing contours of newly fallen snow over stones in the bed of a shallow river bear an astonishing resemblance to human figures. (1964)

71. Melting ice, the return to a warmer season, resulted in this surface pattern on a stream, which has the elements of a human profile. (1961)

The Creatures

72 and 73. Primeval looking iguanas moving across the rocks of Narborough Island in the Galápagos as the evening mist rolls in. The iguana in plate 72 was made to assume almost mammoth proportions through a close-up shot. (1969)

74 and 75. A swarm of flamingos, viewed from an airplane over Lake Huntington, Kenya. More than three million birds were clustered along the volcanic shoreline alive with hot springs. The flamingos go from lake to lake in search, particularly, of certain chemicals which are not always found in the same place. Both photographs were taken with a normal 50-mm. lens and a polarization filter. (1970)

76. Eagle in flight. Moving my camera to follow the bird's path of flight during a high-speed exposure reduced the trees in the background to an abstract pattern which intensifies the impression of motion. (1970)

77. A heron photographed during the last light of evening. The striking silhouette occurred as the bird was coming to a halt before landing on the stump of a tree. My camera was set at 1/500 second at f.2. (1970)

78. A busy cliff in Iceland where gulls breed by the thousands. The use of a long lens enabled me to bring into focus the birds nesting peacefully in the background, while retaining the fluttering motion of the flying gulls nearer to the camera. The result: a dramatic interplay of activity and of proportion. (1965)

79. At a fish hatchery in Kashmir. The water was crystal clear but filled with reflections from the sunlight. To eliminate this distraction I used a polarizing filter, which also helped to bring out the colors. (1968)

80 and 81. Were it not for the respective wonders of the modern aquarium and of fast color film, obtaining pictures of underwater creatures could have developed into a complicated project on its own. These dolphins were photographed through the window of one of the exhibition tanks in the Miami Seaquarium. The available light allowed for an exposure of 1/200 second at f.5.6. (1968)

82. The tenderest aspects of nature are beautifully expressed by the gentle behavior of this sea lion with its young. The smooth outlines of the rocks on which the two are sunning themselves coincide with those of the animals, while the background color is in happy contrast. (1966)

83. Here, in the Miami Seaquarium shark channel, I was able to capture more of a feeling of the mystery of underwater life and to simulate the vastness of the ocean, as one of the

sharks swam swiftly past, dimly, in the semi-distance. (1970)

84 and 85. A giant turtle inching its way across a rock in the Galápagos. It was more than four feet in circumference and must have been at least a hundred and fifty years old. Although many of these huge turtles are to be found in the region, I had to walk for nearly seven hours to find one. The Galápagos Islands are also the breeding grounds for millions of crabs, which in the evening sunlight, and especially after being washed by the sea, take on the strong, lustrous red hue shown in plate 85. (1965)

86 and 87. Few creatures give one more sense of prehistory than crocodiles and hippos. Both these pictures were telephoto shots, made from a small boat along the Nile, near Murchison Falls, where exotic wildlife is still to be found in abundance. (1970)

88 and 89. The animal in plate 88 might at first glance be mistaken for a mammoth. Furthermore, the outline of the mountain in the background clearly suggests the form of a dinosaur, making this whole scene in Kenya belong, or seem to belong, to a time long before the dawn of history. The second photograph, a telephoto shot of a herd of elephants, was made in Uganda at sunset. (1970)

90. Although this herd looks peaceful enough, the buffalo is one of the most dangerous animals in Africa. I took the photograph from a Land Rover, using a telephoto lens. (1970)

91. The Serengeti National Park is famous for its population of lions, which hunt mostly by night and sleep during the day. I took many photographs of this couple in full sunlight, but preferred the quiet mood and color of this daytime shot exposed as a cloud passed overhead. (1970)

92. The wildebeest is often called the clown of the plains. The animals live in big migratory herds, and, whether running or walking, they are always in perfect formation, one after the other. Their movements are well organized, like those of an army. I came upon this group between Serengeti and Masai Mara. (1970)

93 and 94. Two studies of motion. The fleeting images of wild horses galloping across the hot, arid desert land of Nevada are the result of a long exposure, about 1/5 second at f.16. Both pictures were taken in the late afternoon. (1960)

95. Flamingos flying in formation one evening over the dark green water of Lake Huntington. I used a polarization filter to reduce reflections and bring the background into a path of even color. The slow exposure, about 1/5 second at f.11 (using a Leicaflex 400-mm. lens), caught the graceful fluttering movement of the birds' wings. (1970)

96 and 97. In Uganda I spent the best part of a day following a flock of cranes. In plate 96, two birds are flying so close together and in such perfect synchronization that the appearance is of a single bird in flight. While my camera was trained on the cranes, I was suddenly aware of the leaping impala. It was as if this graceful animal had been inspired by the flight of the birds and was trying to compete with them by taking long flying jumps. Both pictures were taken with a Leicaflex 400-mm. lens. (1970)

98 and 99. Two pictures which look as though they might have been photographed a few feet apart were, in fact, separated by many thousands of miles and ten years of time. The herd of graceful impala was taken in East Africa in 1970, and the deer and faun, who are resting in the shade and appear to be holding an intimate conversation, were taken in California in 1960.

100. Perhaps a corner of the Garden of Eden looked like this? For three days working from a small rowboat between the lush green papyrus islands of the Nyasa Lake district, I studied the life and movement of the beautiful Goliath heron. He stands tall and moves slowly and silently in the most colorful of settings. (1970)

101. Late one afternoon I came upon these two baboons along the banks of Lake Manyara and I watched them playing and feeding. There was something very human about the pair, both in their appearance and in the way they reacted to one another. (1970)

102. I followed this Admiral butterfly for a long while before it finally decided to rest on a leaf. I was standing many feet

away, but a 180-mm. Sonnar lens enabled me to get the close-up I wanted. (1965)

103. My intention here was to communicate what a bee sees when it enters a flower in search of nectar. I used a Micro-Nikkor 55-mm. lens, which, in direct opposition to the lens used for plate 102, allows one to photograph an object at very close range. (1965)

104. In the National Park at Nairobi I turned in surprise to find this snake lightly coiled on the spiky branches of a thorn bush. The creature seemed to be suspended in mid-air and to symbolize the magnetism of all the snakes of the world. I photographed it with a 90-mm. Leica lens at a distance of about ten feet. (1970)

105 and 106. Perhaps the most challenging subject in the portrayal of "The Creation" is man. Both these pictures were taken, quite simply, on a sand dune. A gentle wind was blowing, and the rays of the early morning sun hit directly on the two figures side by side in the grass. Plate 105 is a straight shot; plate 106, where the figures are about to arise, is a sandwich photograph, with the image of the sun superimposed. (1970)

ACKNOWLEDGMENTS

This book
is dedicated to my children
Alexander and Victoria

Among those people who have helped me
during its preparation
I am particularly indebted to the following:
Helen Wright
Bryan Holme
Mauro and Marina Filicori
Dan Budnik
and
Quality Color Laboratories

The Story of the Creation,
from Genesis in the Old Testament in the Bible,
follows the
King James Version